JUSTICE WITHIN

DCI Graeme King Book 1

Eddie Newell

Mum.

My inspiration to write.

First Printing: Dec 2018
Amazon KDP

ISBN-9781791921583

Eddie Newell
For details of all books by this author visit his website at

www.eddienewell.com

CONTENTS

Chapter 1. 1

Chapter 2. 3

Chapter 3. 8

Chapter 4. 12

Chapter 5. 17

Chapter 6. 19

Chapter 7. 23

Chapter 8. 25

Chapter 9. 30

Chapter 10. 32

Chapter 11. 35

Chapter 12. 40

Chapter 13. 46

Chapter 14. 52

Chapter 15. 56

Chapter 16. 62

Chapter 17. 67

Chapter 18. 70

Chapter 19. 74

Chapter 20. 85

Chapter 21. 89

Chapter 22...91

Chapter 23...96

Chapter 24. 102

Chapter 25...104

Chapter 26. 110

Chapter 27. 116

Chapter 28. 118

Chapter 29. 121

Chapter 30...124

Chapter 31. 126

Chapter 32...129

just before you go... 131

"*I was no chief and never had been, but because I had been more deeply wronged than others, this honour was conferred upon me, and I resolved to prove worthy of the trust.*"

— *Geronimo*

CHAPTER 1.

The Butterfly Effect;
The phenomenon whereby a minute localized change in a complex system
can have large effects elsewhere.
The name of this theory came to be when a Chaos Theory stated: "It has been
said that something as small as the flutter of a butterfly's wing can ultimately
cause a typhoon halfway around the world."

The wood framed photo proudly on display in the living room, shows a man in his seventies, grey hair, thinning, receding, but not bald. He carries some weight around his middle and the T shirt he wears brandishes the Superman motif as it snuggles and stretches across his protruding, rotund belly. That choice of top alone tells everyone about the sense of fun he has; had. His beaming smile, that involves his whole face, evidences his character and encourages any who view this capture of a moment in time, to laugh along with him. Harry Vaughen was a grandad, dad, husband and longtime railway worker, until his retirement 11 years ago. His passing at 76 was desperately sad for his family, but it was one of those deaths that happen daily and only those close to the deceased are touched by it. Harry had neither sought nor achieved fame and aside from the obligatory, for people of his generation, obituary in the local press, his passing would have largely gone unnoticed.

However, someone had noticed. They had been inconspicuously waiting for an event such as this. Who would have thought the nature of his death was going to shake the foundations of this country to their core. What ordinarily would have been just another person dying, was in fact the catalyst for action by a surprising source. It was as if a key had been inserted into the ignition, the dashboard had lit up and the wheels were now in motion. The aim was clear, the likelihood of success against the might of the political and legal machines was uncertain and as for their future, they were gambling with a hard earned, comfortable life, against the strong possibility of incarceration. For them, to do nothing had ceased being an option a long time ago.

A certain degree of posthumous, unwanted fame was possibly going to be thrust on Harry's family, and that was unfortunate, but the planning to get to this stage had been too arduous and time consuming to miss this opportunity.

The origin of this offensive had been an earlier death, and although Harry died in very different circumstances, his demise had lit the touch paper. As the famous actor of yester year, Kirk Douglas, had once said;

In order to achieve anything, you must be brave enough to fail.

Yes Kirk, yes. Succeed, fail or anywhere in between, this was happening.

CHAPTER 2.

Keep Mum.
To keep silent or quiet.
'Mumming', or 'miming' as it was sometimes called, derives from the word
'mum'. Early versions of mumming involved a parade of characters entering
houses to dance or play games in silence, that is, 'miming'.

As Eloise sat in the waiting area, she glanced down at her shoes to make sure they had not collected any unwanted debris on the journey in. Some fluff was gently extracted off the sleeve of her striped, navy mix, single breasted blazer and any creases brushed out of the matching pencil skirt. For any business meeting she liked to be smart, but not flashy. Her jewellery and watch were demure, and she repeatedly ran her fingers through her layered hairstyle, so it did not appear too brushed.

She guessed that beyond some of the walls she was staring at there would be lots of activity happening, with civil servants carrying out their clerical duties that helped the NHS function as it did. As with all large organisations there was likely to be a mixture of career seekers, doing those extra little bits to stand out, and hopefully one day be rewarded with an office of their own, and of course career enders, there for the money and not likely to do more than was required. Both parties fully understood the other, but it was unlikely they would admit as much openly in conversation. Far more probable was to hear the defence of a position and the criticism of those who might disagree.

Busy little upstart, only cares about what will get them noticed.
Lazy old swine, only ever does the minimum.

Despite having visited the building on a number of occasions, she had never seen the inner workings of this department, just the comfortable office suites and reception rooms of the more senior people. Would the contrast in environment from where she was sitting to the open office areas, be like walking from a private hospital into an NHS ward she pondered?

"Mrs Langley, the Secretary of State will see you now." The aide to the Health Secretary was very pleasant and, as always, acted with total deference to his boss. Smart, black, highly polished shoes, an off the peg suit, white shirt and bland tie, blue on this occasion, were all part of the 'uniform' for civil servants in this department. Clearly this one had the merest element of rebellion in him, as he had hooped socks, radiating all the colours of the rainbow. If he was liked, it would be declared as showing individualism. If less well thought of, those socks might preclude his chances of advancing through the ranks. On the choice of hosiery, careers could be decided. Strange to imagine perhaps, but wretchedly true.

This was the third Secretary of State for Health Eloise had been feted by since the launch of her revolutionary medical breakthrough. It had saved the NHS thousands, millions probably, and contributed to the wellbeing of the nation, so every piece of political advantage that could be gained from it was always sought by those in power. She understood and did not mind at all, as the wholesale adoption by the NHS had contributed to her status as a wealthy woman, not to mention influential. The title of the department changed from time to time, but essentially, they all did the same job. Her husband and business partner, Bob, stayed in the background, where he was more comfortable, so, as the public face of the business, it was her role to press the flesh of health secretaries and the like.

"Eloise, lovely to see you again."

"Secretary."

His handshake was firm and the placing of the left hand over both their hands was well practised. The hand hug as it was called. To some it portrayed honesty and being trustworthy, but in her experience too often the personality behind this particular greeting, lacked the substance to back it up.

"Please, call me John. Sit, make yourself comfy. Tea?"

"No thanks."

John Kuria was of African descent, rightly proud of his ancestry and spoke with the ritzy tones associated with a top class, private school. His father had started a business from scratch, made a go of it, sold it and then moved on to other enterprises. He was wealthy and felt a private education was a sound investment in his son's future. Sadly, any political appointment of ethnicity or colour to high office was still tinged with tokenism, but John Kuria was a smart operator. Intelligent, well connected and came across as humorous and personable when in front of the scrutinous TV cameras. Essential qualities for career minded MPs, as many void of such attributes had found as they grappled with a greasy pole and slithered further and further down the government pecking order. Shaved head, full beard, no tie and a loud orange shirt, under his black suit, made it clear he was confident enough to make a statement with his appearance.

Eloise sat down on one of two ornate chairs facing the desk, but positioned so they were ever so slightly angled into each other. John Kuria sat on the other chair, leaned back and crossed his legs so that one foot was resting on his opposite knee. His elbows rested on his upper thighs and his fingers interlocked. It did not strike her as being overly comfortable, but he seemed very relaxed.

"Let's get to it then. I appreciate much of the preliminary work has been done by my staff, but before pen was put to paper, I wanted to be sure I had spoken to you personally."

"That's completely understandable as this is a considerable financial undertaking by your department. Do you have any concerns?"

His mild frown and crooked grin leaked some surprise at the question.

"Concerns? Absolutely not. I merely want to be sure you are happy with what we are proposing, in terms of money, roll out etc."

"Well, we are not a million miles from tying up all the loose ends and unless you are planning some radical amendments to the contract, everything is more than acceptable from our end."

"No changes from me. My people have done a grand job as far as I'm concerned. I have the one page briefing here." He wagged a finger in the direction of his desk, but did not make any move to indicate he was going to retrieve it. "This will be a moment in history that will be discussed for millennia to come. The parents and legal guardians of all 5 year olds will be offered the implant of your 'Chipsule'. If they accept the offer it will then be provided free of charge. Based on the success of the last 4 years, I think we can expect the uptake to be by the overwhelming majority."

His manner and the excitement in his voice led her to conclude there were no major items to discuss with the contract and roll out. All good news. So why this meeting?

"Forgive me, but if all the ends have been more or less tied up, I'm not sure why you wanted to see me."

He unhooked his legs and stood up.

"Ah yes. Barraclough, would you step outside for a few minutes? Thank you so much."

Still using surnames to talk to staff; really? She wondered if the civil service knew Queen Victoria was no longer alive. Having followed his aide to the door and checked it was fully closed, he sat again, but this time he was more perched on the edge of the seat, which meant he was closer to Eloise.

"That's better, a bit of privacy. Fact is I have some good news for you. What am I saying, it's bloody brilliant news. I have been tipped off that a certain somebody, not sitting that far away from me right now, is likely to be on the next honours list and I wanted to be the one to deliver the news to you."

"Oh, that's.................that is wonderful news. Thank you for taking the time to share that with me. It was very considerate of you."

"I am just so pleased for you. Your work has transformed many forms of medical diagnosis and the cost savings to the taxpayer have been monumental at a time where paying for our health service was a rapidly growing concern. Any award is more than deserved."

"You are very kind."

"One small favour, if you wouldn't mind. I would like to televise the launch of the new agreement and your attendance is going to add considerable gravitas to the whole proceedings."

"If my diary allows, I would be more than willing."

* * *

Eloise hot footed it away from the meeting. Once outside in the square, she spotted a quiet seat away from the main walkways and headed for it. She grabbed her phone out of her bag and rang the most frequently used number. Her husband.

"Bob. You are not going to believe this.......................No, nothing wrong with the deal, in fact it wasn't even about that.................I know.............anyway, they are only going to put me on the honours list...............of course I couldn't accept.......................no...........even if I did accept it, they would only retract once I went public..............yeah, OK....................you realise what this means though? I know it sounds monstrous, but we need someone to die from our list soon............... you are joking.......... who............. Harry Vaughen................ well then, we chat tonight and I visit the local plod tomorrow....... I know, I've gone all goose bumpy...............That's right. For Tobias. Love you."

She held the phone close to her chest as the news sunk in. The emotions of excitement and fear were very powerful and very separate, yet it was hard to distinguish between them. They had waited a long time for this and now it was here. Really here. She wondered how many other people get to have a moment like this, then shamefully realised members of terrorist cells do. They wait for an order, an instruction or a signal of some sort and then all the planning, all the premise of living normal lives, and of course the waiting, it is all over. An event, an occurrence of some sort, was usually the catalyst for those extremist's subterfuge to be concluded. For her it was this poor man's passing. She wondered why that comparison had entered her head and then realised what her subconscious was doing. In the very near future she would be considered a terrorist, of sorts.

To block out that horrid, negative connotation, she began jumping ahead and running through what she would be doing tomorrow. It was real at last. She couldn't wait.

CHAPTER 3.

Apple of My Eye;
Something or someone cherished and loved above all others.
The literal meaning of apple of my eye derives from the fact that in the past
there was no word to describe the pupil of the eye. In those days, they thought
that the pupil was a solid round object which they referred to as an apple, as it
was the most common solid round object at the time. Eyesight was considered
to be something very precious that needed looking after. If someone was 'the
apple of someone's eye' it meant that they were similarly precious and
important. In other words, it was used as a term of endearment to show
someone you really loved or cared for them.

Robert Langley met Eloise McLeod in their second year at University through some mutual friends who felt he might need a nudge to make a move on this girl he had been talking about so much. The way they just happened to be sat together at the local pub curry night was clumsy, but effective in its love-able aim. The choice was long, awkward silences or engage in some chat and find out a bit more about each other. He found out she liked to talk, and she found out he sweated profusely when eating a Lamb Vindaloo. They began going out immediately. He was studying Computer Science and she was taking Biology. They clicked instantly, enjoying a love of sports, music concerts and drinking; lots of drinking. She achieved a first and him a 2.1, which she never failed to remind him of. Post university, they married. They were sure about each other, so why wait any longer. It was a low key, low budget wedding, but outside of the births of the children, it was still their favourite day. He wanted to set up his own computer programming business, so she joined the medical profession and used her salary to fund his start up. At one point she had toyed with the idea of pursuing her education, but she was desperate to support Bob and that meant getting a job. She could always resurrect her academic aspirations in the future. However, she landed in health analysis and enjoyed it. The upscaling of his business came fast as he tapped in early to the millennium bug as a potential problem and subcontracted out a mass of work. He made a fortune and she joined the business. The millennium bug was a cash cow, but it also had a limited shelf life, so whilst Bob looked ahead for other opportunities, Eloise took control of the operation of the business.

They had three children, owned a penthouse flat in the city and a large property in a far more rural setting. Life was good. Eloise stopped working during her maternity leave, but returned to work as soon as she felt she could. She did not need to financially, but being a full time 'mummy' was just not her. She loved her children more than anything, however she also liked her career. Being the boss meant she could manage her time around the needs of the kids, so she never missed a parents evening, a sports match or the magic that is a Christmas play. There will always be those people who are ready, eager even, to scoff and whisper about the choice's others make, but her and Bob were comfortable with the balance they had in their lives.

Eloise had enjoyed her health service experience, but it had not been without its frustrations. Good people, working hard, but hampered by the infrastructure, bureaucracy and people playing politics. There was not enough money being put in by the government. Each new party in power knew that simply putting more cash in now, without radical reforms, would not be money well spent, but how do you turn a liner the size of the NHS around, whilst more and more passengers keep getting on board. It was sinking. To fund it properly in its current guise, would mean significant tax hikes and that was political suicide. Everyone wanted the best health service possible, but too few were prepared to pay any extra to pay for it. So, they muddled along with outdated and costly practices and lengthy diagnosis procedures. This final point was horrible for the patients waiting for results. Most suffered huge swings in emotion, from, it will all be OK, to, what about if they find something really nasty. If it was bad enough for them, for their family it was a nightmare. Walking on eggshells, not sure what to say for the best and running through a myriad of emotions themselves as they waited days for a response. Of course, once they got the results back, the local surgery was mostly focused on the patients who needed further medical support, which meant those who were in the clear might not find out for a few extra days. Blood, and other preliminary tests requiring lab analysis were also expensive to run for the health authority.

Over an evening meal Eloise discussed her latent annoyance on this after a friend had shared the worry she was going through waiting for some blood results on her husband who had collapsed at work. He had recovered, but the test findings would indicate if he was at risk of another such occurrence and give a far clearer idea of the longer term prognosis. Bob was empathetic to her feelings and they decided to seek a remedy, using their joint skillsets. After 7 years of research, multiple failures, or as Thomas Edison said, 'ways that don't work', they came up with the 'Chipsule'. It was an electronic chip that could relay information used in many common forms of diagnosis; white blood cell count, complete blood count, calcium and glucose levels, to name a few. Volunteers would have the Chipsule implanted in them semi-permanently. This meant it was developed to remain in the body, possibly being changed every few years if necessary. The beauty was instant diagnosis, and hopefully reassurance to the patient, of many issues. If further treatment was necessary, at least they immediately knew the outcome and could come to terms with what procedures were required.

The problem that caused the development to take such a long time, had been how to stop the body from rejecting, or breaking down, the chip over time, without hampering the output. They could extract the data by increasing the intensity of the concentrated electrons, but there was a danger of causing unpleasant side effects. The solution was to coat the chips in a revolutionary substance that made it look more like a very small capsule. The term Chipsule was coined by Alice, who was a senior member of staff at Bob's organisation. The item would lie dormant in the body, impenetrable to our protection systems and causing no serious side effects. As the provider of a medical product, they had to declare all the possible physical reactions up front or face the risk of being sued in the future. However, based on the output of a sustained and varied research programme, they were confident any potential secondary responses would be minor in nature and acceptable due to the benefits. Most people can cope with a little nausea or an equivalent level of discomfort. It was likely most people would have the Chipsule placed in their arm, but it was possible to locate it in other areas of the body if more localised information was required.

During the trial period, Bob and Eloise, provided the data extraction devices to GP practices in their local area free of charge, along with all the training on how to use them. The handheld device was placed near the implanted Chipsule and data was fed into the touchscreen tablet, with instant results provided. No volunteer would be asked to rely on the output from the Chipsules as the sole piece of diagnosis, but the results would be compared with the current lab analysis approach. After 6 months, and a 98.7% accuracy strike rate, the government was put under pressure to use the Chipsules nationally by a newspaper campaign. It was revolutionary in its concept. The cost savings and volunteer feedback caught the attention of numerous politicians, because claiming to be part of this was a sure fire vote winner.

Every new Chipsule implanted was recorded on the tablet provided, by Bob's team, to every GP practice and hospital who carried out the procedure. That information was instantly relayed to the central databank located at the business Head Office building. The process was slick, the wellbeing impact a vote winner and the cost savings significant. Any government would invest based on those findings.

A national roll out to all GP practices was agreed and whilst Eloise took charge of the planning, Bob was looking into ways to improve the technology. He set up a team to look at the next generation Chipsules, hardware and tablet software. Eloise and Bob had found the successor to the millennium bug for their business. They were rich already, but now they were considered even more successful and Eloise's fame, in particular, was growing due to news broadcasters' requests for interviews and other TV appearances. Politicians wanted to befriend them. Through invites to exclusive functions they got to know the great and good of the nation and rubbed elbows with fellow rich list names. They had long stopped pinching themselves to confirm this life was actually happening to them. It was the norm. They were used to it and no time was spent on considering how it might ever be different.

Some say the worst part of a rollercoaster ride is being at the highest point, because you know one heck of a drop is going to happen very soon. The rollercoaster of life can disguise or shroud any impending descent, so when it occurs the effect is intensely shocking and the speed with which the ride slows, can cause whiplash to the neurological systems. Those same systems that shape us to be the individuals we are. Without warning, the Gods, the stars and perhaps Mother Nature, contrived to rock Eloise and Bob and the stable world they inhabited. The earth shattering events would give them a new goal, a greater purpose, one that would overshadow everything else. These established pillars of society were to take a different path. They would use their influence, their status and every penny they had, if necessary, to achieve their aim. They felt cheated. They thought the system was corrupt, unfair. They wanted justice.

CHAPTER 4.

A White Elephant;
A burdensome possession; creating more trouble than it is worth.
White (albino) elephants were regarded as holy in ancient times in Thailand
and other Asian countries. Keeping a white elephant was a very expensive
undertaking, since the owner had to provide the elephant with special food
and provide access for people who wanted to worship it. If a Thai King became
dissatisfied with a subordinate, he would give him a white elephant. The gift
would, in most cases, ruin the recipient.

Tobias was the eldest child, followed by Andrew just under 2 years later and then Alana within 18 months. Her birth had been the most difficult and this, along with the glaring awareness of the ageing process, had helped them decide their family was complete. By modern standards it was a largish group and they were blessed with what they had. The whole family were close and it was only when Tobias went to university that they spent any lengthy time apart. His return was always much cause for excitement. Apart from being the eldest, he was also funny, interesting to listen to and interested to find out what everyone else had been up to.
His passing was a shock. No last chance to say good bye, in fact no last anything. There are occasions when death becomes expected, at the finale of a long term illness for example. Even though it is inevitable, when it happens the realisation can still leave the relatives cold, unprepared for the ending. So the totally unexpected death of their son, a healthy young man, was beyond chilling for Bob and Eloise. It was also crushing for Andrew and Alana, who up to that point in their tender years had never, thankfully, experienced the pain of losing someone so close. Tobias was out with some friends for a lunchtime drink and when walking home a car had hit him, death was instant. The zebra crossing clearly gave him priority right of way, but the motorist did not see him, did not decelerate and collided with him at a speed of 38 mph. It was a 30 mph area. Tobias was leading the pack as he stepped onto the

black and white stripes. He had glanced right and left, and as some cars began slowing, dipping front ends indicating braking, he took that as his cue to stride out. Who knows how he did not see the car heading his way; perhaps he had not looked hard enough, perhaps the Subaru was blocked. Whatever the reason, it was of little consequence.

The fact it was just him who had been hit was the only blessing that could be extracted from the whole incident, as the boyfriend and girlfriend who were following Tobias were inches from being struck. Eyewitnesses said he was thrown through the air and landed on his head. The police think he was dead as soon as the initial impact was made, so hopefully the few seconds before his head came into contact with the tarmac were not while he was conscious.

A breathalyser reading taken at the accident site had revealed the driver, Jonas Rafferty, had alcohol in his system over 5 times the legal limit. His Subaru WRX STI, with a 2.5 litre turbo petrol engine, was perhaps evidence to the way he liked to drive. Apparently, he was upset for what had happened, but not overly remorseful. He came from money, a long history of money, and, whether intentionally or not, he gave the impression this meant he was better than other people. Daddy's wealth had provided some of the best legal representation possible, which seemed a bit pointless in view of the nature of the offence and overwhelming evidence. However, Reginald Rafferty was of the opinion that everything really does have a price and for the sake of his son, he was prepared to pay as much as was needed.

Whether it was the expensive lawyer, a friendship, albeit a bit distant, with the regions Chief Constable or just that money talks, it was incredible, verging on the unbelievable, that a technicality was unearthed with the way the police had recorded the evidence. Jonas was no longer on trial for manslaughter, just dangerous driving. Instead of facing life as a maximum sentence, his worst case scenario now was 5 years. As if that was not bad enough, the defence then cast Tobias as the cause of his own death.

Admittedly, it was a zebra crossing, but there still lies a responsibility on any pedestrian to make sure they can safely cross the road. This clearly did not happen on that fateful day. Tobias had been drinking with his friends, so perhaps his senses were dulled and that affected his ability to judge the speed and distance of the oncoming car.

The sentence was 2 years and it was likely Jonas would be out much sooner than that. As Bob and Eloise left the Courthouse, the parents and family of Jonas were openly celebrating; two years was nothing to what they had braced themselves for. The whooping, cheering and joyous, tearful, hugging was played out totally oblivious to the feelings of anyone else and insensitive to the memory of Tobias, who they were effectively stomping all over. Bob could not contain himself, he marched up to the father. His face was red, his fists were clenched and the passion in his voice did nothing to hide his disgust and anger.

"You do realise my son died at the hands of yours. I do not think this is the time, the place or the occasion to be congratulating yourselves." He was right in the face of Reginald Rafferty. Amid his excitement this was the last thing he had expected, it came out of nowhere. But, his feeling of euphoria was not going to be deflated by anyone.

"I am sorry for your loss, but both our sons had been drinking, so who is to say it was not six of one and half a dozen of the other as to who is to blame? My son is not going to prison for as long as we first thought and whether you wish to understand how that feels or not is up to you, but it is the best news ever for us."

"Your son is to blame, totally to blame. He was drunk at the wheel of a high powered vehicle and he killed my son. There is no good news in that. I am telling you to do your gloating in private or I may not be responsible for my actions."

"Really? Look, why not join us for a drink and let's put this whole thing behind us."

"Are you insane?"

"The accident happened months ago and carrying it around with you like this cannot be doing you any good. Accidents happen. It's time to move on."

"We can never move on from the death of our son."

"That's your choice. Now if you don't mind, my family and friends are waiting for me and I could do with a drink."

Eloise had heard the exchange and came close.

"Mr Rafferty, you are a prize piece of shit. Enjoy your moment of happiness, because I intend to make you, and that useless son of yours, rue the day you danced on my son's grave."

As she broke her glare from Reginald, she viewed the rest of those who had been celebrating with him. She knew what Carla Rafferty looked like from the papers and the brief eye contact between them told Eloise that Carla was not entirely comfortable with the situation she found herself in. Other people were starting to notice this side show, so Eloise grabbed Bob by the arm and firmly led him away. He submitted to her dragging, but kept his eyes firmly locked on Reginald Rafferty, who for his part shook his head a bit and then rallied those around him, who had been silenced by the flare up between the two men, and they headed off to the nearest bar. There it was, the moment when Eloise knew what she had to do. They would forever grieve for Tobias, but now she had a new drive in her life. Jonas Rafferty would pay for his crime and his family could feel the same despair as Bob and she had.

The next couple of days were spent having some precious family time and coming to terms with a second bout of grief, brought on by the trial reliving the end of Tobias's life in intricate detail. They had grieved at the news of his death. Above the family, heavy, dark clouds formed to block out the strains of light that could reveal hope, and with no acknowledgement of the merest hint of a fair wind to blow them away, the murkiness remained constant until well after the funeral. Gradually, they began to tolerate the slow, but perpetual shifting of time as it slightly dampened their pain, heading for a point way into the future where it might just become bearable. Then, months down the line, the hurt was unearthed again. They were back to square one; well almost. What anyone touched by the loss of a loved one knows, is that there comes a time to get some normality back in their lives or spend forever being consumed by that loss. The departed would loathe the waste of a life that would be. Bob returned to work, Andrew to 6th form and Alana to school. Eloise had taken a few extra days off; the team around her had been great about it and she took advantage of their kindness in full knowledge of how capable they were, with or without her. She needed some space if she was going to come up with a way to make those bastards sorry.

Then it came to her. Yes, Reg and Jonas would suffer, but her plan was far more encompassing than just those prats. A man, driving under the considerable influence of alcohol, speeding, not taking due care for pedestrians and who had robbed another young man of his life, should not be free in, potentially, a matter of months. The system was to blame. For every grinning Reginald Rafferty picture, she saw in her mind, there was a judge, senior police official, lavish living lawyer or politician coming into her view. She breathed deeply, lifted her coffee mug up to a photo of Tobias and made a pledge; I will bring their old boy network, funny handshake, crooked system down with a massive bang. Perhaps some greater being had chosen her specifically for this task. If so, they would not be disappointed.

As Reg Rafferty cried for what had happened to his son, she would sip champagne in his face. The scene was playing out in her mind;

It's time for you to move on Reg, so would you join me in a glass of champers? No! Well, that's your choice. Now if you don't mind, my family and friends are waiting for me and I could do with a drink.

A certain warmth emanated from somewhere within and slowly transmitted itself to every part of her as she watched the imagery in her head. The sound of her voice aping his intonation, the sight of his face as veins pumped red dye over his features and the feeling, oh that feeling, of knowing he could taste the bitterness of his own words.

She knew there would be occasions when her spirits may need lifting once she began this quest, so she had started collecting quotes that she could read to energise her mind if the darkness loomed. The page was open on one by Martin Luther King, Jr;

Human progress is neither automatic nor inevitable... Every step toward the goal of justice requires sacrifice, suffering, and struggle; the tireless exertions and passionate concern of dedicated individuals.

The justice he desired was perhaps of a different nature, but his words reached out to her. She made a mental note to capture this moment and bank it, ready to be drawn upon if, and when, necessary. The warmth became a glow.

CHAPTER 5.

Bee in your bonnet;
To be totally obsessed with something.
The origin of the phrase is believed to be a variant of the 16ᵗʰ century
expression, to have bees in the head, which was used to imply scatiness. John
Heywood, a poet and court musician, made the link between bees and crazed
thought in his collection of English proverbs, printed in 1546. Perhaps the
Scottish twist was to replace head with their favourite form of headwear, the
bonnet.

Bob was worried. Eloise had called him at work and wanted him to come home as soon as possible. With the mental turmoil they were all suffering this could mean anything, and she was giving no clues away during the call. He tidied up a few loose ends and headed home, stopping once to buy some flowers for her. He had no idea about flora, so he asked for a bouquet that would cheer someone up. £35 later he was in possession of a large, multicoloured, seasonal bouquet.

"Oh Bob, they are lovely. Thank you. I'll put them in the sink in water for now and sort them later." She kissed him on the lips. The affectionate, quick caress, so many couples use in place of hello or goodbye. Their kiss was always laden with feeling, never token or mundane, but on occasions it felt different. Today was such an occasion. The affection was there, but he sensed she was distracted. He followed her into the kitchen.

"What's up then?"

"I thought afterwards that I might have panicked you a bit with my call. Sorry if I did."

"You did."

"Andrew and Alana shouldn't be home until 6 and I wanted to explain what I'm going to do and thought we needed a few hours to agree everything. I hope you'll join me."

17

"Join you in what?"

"I am going to take on the system. Jonas bloody Rafferty and that fathead of a father of his will seem to be the focus of my attention, and have no doubts they will suffer, but actually I am after much bigger fish."

"Eloise, I have to ask, are you up to this? I can hardly think at work sometimes as I'm feeling grief, guilty of course and mostly just plain angry. Shouldn't you get back to work and see how you cope before taking on the world?"

"Yes, I should. Then again, you should have got a job like everyone else when you left uni, but you didn't and look where we are today. We should probably have given up on the Chipsule after the knockbacks for the first few years, but we didn't. Look how that has panned out. Neither of us have got to where we are today by doing what we should. Wait until you hear what I'm thinking and then see if you think I will be able to cope."

"Don't need to. If it means that much to you, and if it is within my power, I will go along with whatever you want. With one proviso. If it starts to affect Andrew and Alana, you will have to count me out. We were custodians of three other lives and we have lost one of those. I will protect them with every ounce of my being. I love you, however, I know how wrapped up in projects you get and this sounds like being the biggest yet. I will choose their wellbeing over your crusade, any and every day."

"I would demand that of you. Have no worries as they are built in to the plan."

"Come on then, hit me with it."

"Let me give you a big picture version and then I'll fill in the details. When the time comes, you and Alana are going a long way away, Andrew will stay here to carry on with his A levels, but be kept at a safe distance from any hassle. I am going to give myself in to the police based on potentially many murders and I will be making incredible demands of the authorities. I will become infamous and will be risking my liberty."

"Sounds simple enough! Remind me why you are doing this?"

"Tobias was murdered. His killer will be free to roam the streets anytime soon and probably will be drink driving straightaway, meaning another family could be made to suffer like us. Problem is, because of money and a messed up, useless system, people like Jonas don't have to worry. Why am I doing this? I want to stop Reg grinning. I want to stop lawyers finding technicalities for guilty people in return for huge paydays. Most of all I have the means to make some noise, unlike so many households up and down this country, so I am doing this for them. I want a justice system that lives up to its name."

CHAPTER 6.

Let the cat out of the bag;
Disclose a secret.
Relates to the fraud of substituting a cat for a piglet at markets. If you let the
cat out of the bag you disclosed the trick - and avoided buying a pig in a poke
(bag). This form of trickery is long alluded to and 'pigs in a poke' are recorded
as early as 1530.

The police station was a modern building, reddish burgundy brickwork and lots of
reflective glass. The police do not want us seeing what happens inside, thought
Eloise. You stupid woman, this is not some Soviet bloc country or dictatorship. Get a
grip or heaven knows what you will be like once inside. As she approached the main
door she checked out her appearance in one of the mirror glass panes. Why on earth
am I doing that, it's not a fashion show. She pressed a buzzer and the officer
manning the front desk looked up and flicked some switch that let her in.
"Hello. I'd like to speak to someone about a possible suspicious death please."
"May I ask why you think it could be suspicious?"
"I would prefer to speak to someone in a less public space if you don't mind."
"Very well, I will see if one of the detectives is available."
"Your name please."
"Eloise Langley."
"Ah. I thought I recognised your face. Please take a seat. There is water available
from the cooler over there."
"Thank you."
She sat down on a cloth covered seat. I wonder what manner of naughty bums have
been on here ahead of me, she thought. The desk officer had disappeared, probably
not wanting to make a call in front of her. She looked around the waiting area. There
was a young man in jeans and a grey hoodie, head slumped over his knees, so she
couldn't make out much of his face. Probably reporting in as part of his probation

she guessed. The only other person was a stern looking lady, probably in her 40s or 50s, who had her arms crossed and was sitting back in her seat, legs straight out in front of her with one over the other. She looked rough, hard, but also worn out. Perhaps here to find out what they've done with one of her 8 out of control children, Eloise mused. Then a door opened and out came man in a suit, shiny through wear. The lady stood up, they kissed and headed out together. A copper's wife. Eloise reproached herself, funny how the minute you enter a place like this and you think the worst of everyone.

"Mrs Langley?"

"Yes."

"Would you like to come through please."

He held the door for her and then moved ahead so she could follow him. He was smart in appearance, with a newish looking dark blue suit, checked blue and white shirt and a plain purple tie. Well polished brown brogues and a chunky silver watch completed his look. He was dark haired, but grey flecks were emerging. She guessed he was in his 30s. He opened a door to an interview room and she was greeted by a lady, who rose and they shook hands. He then did the same. "Sorry." If Bob was there instead, would he have shaken hands at the door? His co-interviewer gave him a sideways look as if to say 'prat'. The woman might have been slightly older than him, but not much, although the way she carried herself suggested she was the senior officer. Cream blouse, grey jacket with the sleeves fashionably rolled up to just below the elbow, black trousers and shoes. She was mixed-race and had very short hair. No necklace or bracelets and even the watch she wore was plain, functional. It was there to tell her the time, rather than make a statement about her fashion sense. Put it all together and it told Eloise this woman was a focused professional with little concern for what people thought of her beyond how she did her job. The wedding band was the only clue to her life that her appearance gave away.

"Please take a seat. This is the only room free at present, hope you don't mind."

"Not at all."

Not being an authority on police interview rooms, Eloise had no idea why the lady was apologising.

"I'm Detective Sergeant Tim Harrison and this is Detective Inspector Rebecca Blades. I understand you want to discuss a suspicious death, is that right?"

"Yes. First of all, thank you for seeing me at such short notice, both of you. I hope this doesn't sound too conceited, but do you know who I am and about my work? If so, it might just save some time."

DI Blades spoke. "I think it's fair to say we know a bit about you and what you do, many officers here, and their families, have had a Chipsule implanted. Not sure how that has anything to do with a suspicious murder though."

"Were you also aware I lost a son when he was hit by a drunk driver?"

"Yes. It was big news at the time. I'm sorry, that must have been terrible for you."

"It was. It still is. We miss Tobias terribly." The tears came from out of nowhere at the mention of his name. She sat up straight, swallowed and got her mind back on why she was there. "The Chipsules, as they have been called, are currently in approximately 5.3 million people across the nation and obviously more people are seeking access to them daily. The death I'm here to report could be down to poison from one of the Chipsules."

Tim Harrison was confused.

"Mrs Langley, if there is a malfunction with your product, do the health authorities know?"

"Forgive me, I haven't explained myself very well. There is no fault with the Chipsules. If the death I am here to report was down to the Chipsule, then who says it was due to a malfunction? What about if I activated something within the Chipsule? What about if I can poison people with them? Millions, upon millions of people."

The detectives looked at each other. DI Blades looked at Eloise.

"I will need to consult with my superiors on how we proceed, but whatever happens this will be a formal interview from now on. I presume you have a legal representative and you might want to let them know what you are doing."

"I will not be needing a lawyer or solicitor at this stage, but I presume I have the right to change my mind at any point. One thing, before you talk to your bosses. I will not allow you to arrest me, detain me or anything of that manner. To do so will mean you, the police, could be putting countless lives at risk."

Both the detectives stood up and then DS Harrison said;

"I'm not sure if I have got my head round this yet, so just to be clear on what's happening. You are saying you have been involved in a suspicious death and you might possibly use your Chipsules to kill a load more people. You, I believe, are then threatening that if we follow normal protocol you will place any deaths caused through that at our door. Is that a decent summary?"

"I have not claimed to be involved in any death as of yet, I have merely been scene setting."

DI Blades frowned. Usually she was in control when conducting interviews, but this woman had landed a bombshell, said she would not accept being detained and seemed relatively calm. Expressing some emotional tendencies, but overall calm, considering the substance of her revelations. Without flouting the rules governing such interactions, could DI Blades prise a bit more information out before heading upstairs?

"You are throwing away your life here, why?"

"I do not believe I am throwing anything away. Are you a mother Detective Inspector

Blades?"

"Yes."

"Imagine, if you can, your child being taken away from you by a callous act and then the system conspiring against you, denying you a chance to move on. The counsellors call it closure and without it, the grieving just goes on and on. Time can heal some of the pain, but it cannot lessen the anger I feel. Imagine the murderer of your child laughing in your face, because his daddy can pay for him to get away with anything. Imagine the damage to your relationship with your husband and how you try to explain what has happened to your other children. I hope you never have to do anything other than imagine all of that. What will be, will be, but I do not consider I am throwing my life away. As a mother you will know that you would do anything for your children and based on the situation I have been forced into, for me, that means in life and beyond. For Tobias, I will have justice."

She was welling up again. It was when she said her son's name out loud, that broke her every time. A distraction was needed to prevent full on crying;

"Do I wait here?"

"Please. I'm sorry, but I'm not sure how long we will be. Would you like some coffee?"

"That would be very nice, thank you."

"It tastes like cardboard, so I wouldn't thank me too much."

The two ladies shared a grin.

"I have heard what you said, but I sincerely hope you have thought about the consequences of your actions."

"I have thought about little else."

CHAPTER 7.

My ears are burning;
You think that other people are talking about you.
This idiom originates from the ancient Romans who believed that different
feelings in the body were signs of current or future events. They thought that a
ringing or burning feeling in the ears was a sign that the person was being
talked about. They also believed that a burning left ear was a symbol of evil
(people were saying bad things about them) and a burning right ear was a
symbol of praise (people were saying nice things about them).

DS Tim Harrison waited until they were through a couple of doors.

"What the hell is going on? What should we do?"

"Tim, I think it is highly unlikely you or me will have anything more to do with this. Big case, celebrity, career maker and all that. Let's tell Graeme and see from there."

Detective Chief Inspector Graeme King, was a tough, old school cop, doing his best to come to terms with the modern, politically correct way of policing the general public and managing his team. It was a struggle. Thankfully, his officers accepted his odd bit of cloddish, verbal, sexism, racism and any other number of ism's as they knew it had no malice and was just him shooting his mouth off. He did not always think before speaking, but he was neither a degenerate or bigot. As his multi-cultural team of both sexes, and varying sexualities, would testify, he was a man you wanted to work for. Nobody is perfect, and they accepted his imperfections in preference to working for someone else. There was a rumour one officer had let on he intended raising a grievance against DCI King, but such was the force of personal negativity to the potential accuser, the gripe itself never went ahead. His guvnors also turned a blind eye as he was a good cop and got results. Graeme knew that when his time was up his old-fashioned ways would be the 'excuse' used to get rid of him.

He was balding, pot-bellied, had the need for reading glasses and was one of those people who could make a designer suit look scruffy. Love him or loathe him, Graeme

King was a straight talking, no nonsense kind of man. His hunched posture meant physically he permanently seemed to be carrying the worries of the world on his shoulders, but that was deceiving. It was a stressful job; however, he had learned how to cope with it over the years. One of the things his subordinates appreciated the most about their DCI was how he did his best to keep the strain off his team as much as was humanly possible. Less appreciated, but indulged, was his attempts at humour. They might not be funny, but he always had a quip ready. The best laid plans for DCI's are often thrown to the wind as the shift unfolds and his day was about to take an unexpected turn.

CHAPTER 8.

Armed to the teeth;
Fully prepared or equipped.
The term armed to the teeth is used to describe someone who is heavily
armed. The origin of this phrase is Port Royal Jamaica from the 1600's and is
considered a "pirate" phrase. Since many of the weapons used by pirates at
this time relied upon a single shot of black powder pirates would have to carry
multiple weapons to protect themselves in a fight. Commonly one of these
weapons was a knife that was carried between their teeth.

Rebecca took the lead with Tim following close behind. He had no idea what he was going to add to what she would say, but he wanted to be there for entertainment value if nothing else. She tapped on the open door and DCI King replied without even looking up.

"Yes Rebecca, what can I do for you?"

"Boss, I've got a really weird one to deal with and I need to know how you want me to play it."

"Come on then, let's hear it."

"Do you know who Eloise Langley is?"

He removed his glasses, placed them on the pad in front of him, rubbed his eyes and then looked up.

"It might surprise you to know my age does not cut me off from what is happening in the world. I have seen her on my black and white portable or perhaps I heard her on my wireless."

"Funny boss, really funny. Anyway, she is in Interview Room 3 right now."

He sat back in his chair, his interest pricked enough to give her his full attention.

"Go on."

"The desk sergeant asks us to see her as she wants to discuss a suspicious death in private. Tim and me think it's nothing more than a discussion and then she lands a big one on us. She indicates she might be responsible for this suspicious death and there could be more to follow."

"Have you charged her?"

Rebecca Blades looked at DS Harrison. He shrugged his shoulders. Well, thank you for that massive display of support Tim.

"No!"

"No!" His echo of her word was loud and verging on incredulous.

"Boss, if we do, she more or less said people would die if she was arrested. Being a big celebrity and all, I thought I had best tread careful."

"First of all, you're a wimp. Secondly, you did exactly what I would have done. Harrison Ford, what was your part in all this?" DCI King liked his little jokes at his team's expense.

"It's Tim, boss. I was interviewing with DI Blades."

"Right, Tim Nice-But-Dim, what do you think we should do?" It was obvious DS Harrison was listening in for the sport of it all, so Graeme thought he would make him the sport.

"Well, I......"

"Come on man, you want to be a DCI one day, don't you?"

"Yes!"

"Then show me you have the balls to be one. What would you do if you were me?"

"I...I...I would interview her myself."

"So, you would give in and indulge her self-importance ahead of all your other non-celebrity cases?"

"That's not...."

"Is that your phone I hear ringing, DS Harrison?"

"No. I don't think so." DI Blades grinned at him and the penny dropped. "So it is. I'll leave you to it."

"Come in Rebecca and shut the door. Why can't I just call you Becky?"

"For the same reason I stopped you calling me Razor; I don't like it."

"Aren't you a little bit too precious to work in a police station?"

"Aren't you a little bit too old?"

"Yes, and still your boss. Tell me what you think."

"You should speak to her. I'll lead, but you should listen in. This one could go all ends up, I just have that feeling. She is super calm and very sure of what she wants. Do you think you should tip off the brass above you?"

"And say what exactly? Let's go see her and then I'll decide what to do."

Graeme put his crumpled jacket on and fiddled with his tie as if to straighten it, but the outcome was only marginally better than it had been. He held out an arm to indicate to DI Blades for her to lead the way and he followed. He shouted down the room of detectives;

"If anyone wants me, I'm interviewing with the person who insists on being called by her full first name, Reeebeca..ca..ca." A big woo went up and DI Blades bowed slightly as she walked. He carried on, "Take any messages and I'll get back to whoever wants me once I'm done, or I might go on a long holiday, or I might be put on gardening leave, or......." His voice dwindled out as the door closed behind him.

* * *

Eloise was lost in her thoughts, so the opening of the door to the interview room by DI Blades startled her a little.

"Hello again, this is DCI Graeme King." He leaned forward, and they shook hands, Eloise remained seated.

"I have given DCI King a brief summary of our discussion, but would you like to provide us with some more details of why you have come forward?"

"Certainly. Before I do that, I realise that some of the demands I will be making could put you in a difficult position and I would rather not do that. Equally, I do not want you to think I'm too up myself, but would it be better for you both if I made my demands aware to someone more senior?"

DCI King responded. "I will reserve the right to be offended." He paused. There was a twinkle in her eye, so his remark had landed as intended. "Did you have anyone particular in mind?"

"Yes, actually. The Health Secretary is something of an acquaintance and whilst this is not really his bag, I thought he might discuss it with the Home Secretary."

"They are some pretty big names to be calling on. OK, I'm impressed."

"I was not out to impress you. I am under no illusions that what I am about to do will stir up one hell of a hornet's nest and I thought it only fair that you appreciate what you're getting into."

"The problem is, I am unsure what it is I'm getting into. If it's alright with you, I would like to decide a course of action, and who to involve, once I know what you have to say and what you want?"

"Of course."

"Can I have your permission to tape our conversation, even though you have not been cautioned, charged or arrested?"

"Of course, I certainly intend to." Eloise rustled about in her bag and produced a digital voice recorder. She placed it on the table, right in the centre. "Ready when you are."

DCI King indicated to DI Blades to load up the recording system by waving a hand and flicking his fingers in the general direction of the machine. She took two tapes out of their cellophane wrapping and loaded them into the unit. She looked at DCI King, he nodded and she pressed the record button.

"This is Detective Inspector Blades and I am being accompanied by Detective Chief Inspector King, we are both officers at Heatfield Police Station. Also present is, please state your name…"

"Mrs Eloise Langley."

"It is the 18th March and the time is 11.47am. Mrs Langley, you arrived at this station to discuss what you described as a suspicious death and have since indicated you may have been involved in this death. Would you care to elaborate?"

"Yes. In my bag I have an envelope containing the name of the person in question, along with his personal information so you can verify what I say. His cause of death will be recorded as 'natural causes'. His medical records will show that one of the data extraction chips, produced by a business I own with my husband, often referred to as Chipsules, was implanted in him about 2 years ago. I may have the ability to effect something within the chips, which let's say is not good for people's health."

"Are you saying you killed this person?" DI Blades was a copper. She wanted certainty.

"Well, here's the thing. Possibly."

"Possibly!" Synchronised wording and heightened pitch inflection from the detectives.

"Yes, possibly. What I'm talking about is unlikely to show up as a cause of death, so I don't know if this person died through natural or intended causes."

DCI King was starting to understand where this was going.

"How many of these chips do you have this power of life and death over?"

"All I can say is, at the last count, there are around 5.3 million Chipsules implanted in patients. That number is obviously growing daily."

"Are you telling me you intend to kill 5.3 million people?"

"Absolutely not."

"How many then?"

"That depends. As I have already advised DI Blades and her colleague earlier, if you attempt to arrest or detain me, lives could be put at risk. If my demands are not met, lives could be put at risk. The number of potential deaths sits with you and whoever else is a decision maker to do with this."

The mention of her name prompted Rebecca Blades to speak.

"Surely any number of deaths sits with you, and you alone?"

Eloise focused on DI Blades. Her body stayed rigidly in position, but her head slowly turned to face the more junior officer. She was controlled, but forceful in her speech.

"That depends entirely on your perspective."

Graeme King felt the tension. He understood why Rebecca said her piece, but this lady was not being formally interviewed, so her intervention was premature. He broke the momentary silence.

"Demands? You said demands. You're sounding a bit like a terrorist. As you will know neither the police nor the government will be held hostage to demands, but for the record, can you tell me what your demands are?"

"DCI King, I've done some research on you and I was led to believe you were a straight talker, so let's engage in some of that shall we? Both you and I know no-one is going to admit to negotiating with criminals, but we also know it happens. Probably quite frequently."

His experience had enabled him to hide his emotions, but he was visibly prickled by what she had said.

"Can I rewind just a little? What do you mean by, done some research on me?"

"I checked who was the senior detective here, assumed you would be involved and as I like to be prepared, I got someone to ask around about you."

"Did you now. Can I ask who did the digging?"

"Of course you can, but I won't tell you. It was a private investigator. Did a good job. Most importantly to me, was that I could deal with someone of integrity. Despite some of your disciplinary matters, and of course the odd muffled grievance, everything they uncovered said you were a man I could trust to do the right thing."

"I have no idea how to respond to that. Thank you for your faith in me, but I am not overly happy at being investigated in this way. Some of that stuff is very personal and not in the public domain, so I may well want to know how this person got that information."

"Well you won't get a name from me. Money and alcohol loosen many a tongue amongst police rank and file I understand. DI Blades must be as uncomfortable as you with this discussion, so shall we move things on? I would be very agreeable to you handling my case, but, as I have already said, you can nudge me along if you felt that was more appropriate."

She reached into her handbag and produced an A4, brown envelope, which she placed on the table.

"Before I reveal any of my requirements, does that sound less terrorist-y to you, I would like you to check out the death of this man for anything suspicious. If you can't find anything, which you are unlikely to, please ask his family or his doctor if there were any notable changes in his health leading up to his death. I think some credibility is more likely to make people listen."

DCI King picked up the envelope and on the front was a name; Harry Vaughen.

CHAPTER 9.

Get one's goat;
To anger or upset someone.
The phrase originated from cows, due to an old belief that keeping a goat in the barn had a calming effect on the cows, who would then produce more milk. Thus, an enemy "getting one's goat" would upset the cows and cause them to be less productive.

DCI Graeme King strode upstairs to his office alone, as Eloise needed a toilet break and he left DI Blades to escort her. As he entered the main open office area where his detectives worked, one or two made a beeline for him as they clearly wanted to discuss something. A sharp, "Not now," accompanied by a scowl was enough to let them reconsider the urgency of their discussion.

He closed his office door behind him, sat down in his chair and faced the wall. He wanted no distractions for a few minutes whilst he got his head together. What the hell did he do now? This was one smart lady. He was slightly irked by her background check on him through a private eye, and extremely displeased that the information had been obtained from fellow officers from his station. That was for another time as he was long enough in the tooth to not let personal feelings get in the way of an investigation. He shook his head and inadvertently permitted a smirk to emerge. Perhaps one or two police families had enjoyed a few extra luxuries last Christmas off the back of dishing the gossip on him. He did not blame them, but that would not stop him trying to find out who it was, in due course.

Is that what this was, an investigation? She wanted him to look into one death, but was indicating there could be more, many more. In fact, she was talking about the potential to wipe out as many people as lived in the whole of Scotland. But, as of yet, it was unsure if the death of this Harry Vaughen was routine or not. If he followed

procedure and had her arrested, apparently that could cause more people to die.
There was a knock on the door, it was Rebecca Blades. He waved her in.

"Is our guest comfortable now?"

"Yeah. What the hell boss. Have you managed to decide what we should do?"

"Unless you have a better suggestion, I think I should involve my highly paid senior officers."

"Too bloody right."

"In the meantime, get looking into this Harry guys death. All the details you'll need are in that envelope; address, next of kin, GP etc. See what you can find out, but gently does it with the family. Use Tim if you need some help. Do it now and let me know as soon as you know anything."

"OK. By the way, have fun when you phone your friend Jezza."

"Naff off, you evil witch."

Superintendent Jeremy Day was not someone DCI King would describe as a friend and the less he needed to involve him in his day to day work the better. They clashed, often. Supt Day had shot up the ranks, using his qualifications, his intellect and his networking skills to extremely good effect. On the way, his hands had rarely been soiled with normal police business, as he had managed to get himself on various projects, courses and was more than happy to attend any meetings that were going. His CV was impressive, the names of influential senior police personnel in his phone contacts was enviable and the breadth of his knowledge on policing matters was second to none. For some, the classroom and workshops were no replacement for live action when it came to being a leader. How could they possibly understand what normal policing involved? Only problem was, those people do not decide on promotions. As his experience was more observational than first-hand, he was a by the book kind of copper. This was in stark contrast to many of the men and women he was line managing, as they relied on an instinct developed through years of dealing with cunning lowlifes, crackheads and all manner of criminal types. Whether he liked it or not, this call had to be made. Graeme's first attempt was met by voicemail, so he contacted the superintendent's office and was told he was meeting with a community group, to do with an increase in the use of knives on a local estate. Yes, he would be asked to call back and yes, he would know it was urgent, but it was likely to be a couple of hours.

His phone rang, it was the desk sergeant downstairs.

"Graeme, Mrs Langley would like to know if it is OK for her to leave and get some lunch and a coffee."

"She what? Would she like her bed folded down and chocolate on her pillow too?" Was she intentionally winding them up? Nah, based on what he had seen earlier, that was probably what she would expect. Through the fog of his brief annoyance he saw an opportunity. "Actually, tell her yes.........as long as I can tag along."

CHAPTER 10.

Break the ice.
To break down social formality and stiffness.
Ships, known as ice-breakers, were equipped with strengthened hulls and powerful engines and were employed in the exploration of polar regions. Soon after these ships were introduced the term 'ice-breaker' began to be applied to social initiatives intended to get strangers acquainted with one another.

The coffee house, Big Mug, was local, produced good coffee and had plenty of seating space. The owner, Val, knew DCI King as a regular customer and eyed his partner for this trip. Too classy for a cop, out of his league and surely he wasn't interviewing criminals off site now? They had agreed to grab a coffee first and then find a meal deal at the small supermarket on the way back to the station. Flat white for her and double espresso for him. He led her to a remote corner away from prying ears and interested eyes.

"Do you bring all your girls here?" she teased.

"As your private investigator will already have told you, the only 'girl' is my wife of 27 years. I have never considered asking her if she would mind me putting myself about a bit, but I'm confident she'd tell me to stop being a silly old man."

"She sounds very sensible, but you're not that old."

"The 'that' in your sentence says so much. So, Mrs Langley..."

"Can we use first names away from the Police Station please? Mine is Eloise."

"We can, mine is Graeme. Now, you to me, what the heck are you doing?"

She swallowed a gulp of coffee. Then slowly, precisely, put the cup back on its saucer. She placed both hands together in her lap.

"I have known the love of a brilliant man, I have known what it is to be a mother to three children and I have known the good life; we do not want for very much as my husband and I have been very successful in business. What I have not known is justice for the unnecessary and cruel death of my son, Tobias."

"May I ask what your husband feels about your visit to the station today?"

"My husband and I no longer live together."

"Oh. I'm sorry."

"It's OK. Grief is not easy to live with and the strain it puts on relationships can be unbearable." She glanced down and played with the handle of her cup. It was fleeting. Then she was on full alert again as she straightened her back, lifted her head and extended her neck to its full length. No residue of any woe in those eyes, just steely determination.

"I'm sure I am not the only person who feels they have been wronged by our legal system, so what I am doing is for them, as much as for me."

"I doubt they would want you to commit murder to pursue a cause, and certainly not in their name."

"Spoken like someone who has not suffered as I have and many others have. If I did not feel I could carry the weight of public opinion with me, then I would not have begun this."

"Mrs Lang.........Eloise, are you really capable of taking the lives of other people? What you have discussed so far will make you a mass murderer on a previously unheard of scale."

She did not blink, she just stared deep into him with cold, bitter eyes.

"I will do whatever I have to, in order to have justice for my son's death."

He was inclined to believe her. Those eyes, that look, this was someone who was set on a path. He slurped his Espresso and contemplated the situation. Perhaps it was the impersonal nature of the way the murders would be carried out that was allowing him to accept her as credible. She was not going to shoot or stab anyone. There would be no blood and gore to deal with. She would not know her victims, I mean who knows millions of people? She had indicated the Chipsules could be used as the lethal weapon. He picked up his mobile phone and texted DI Blades, excusing himself for doing so. *Get Tim to find out all he can about her Chipsules.*

"What exactly is it you want?"

"I told you. Justice."

"Which, in my long experience, can mean many things to many people. What do you, mean by it?"

She scoffed. His tone was serious, but he was fishing. Just hoping she might let her guard down and she saw it a mile off.

"Graeme, I don't drop my knickers that easily. Did you think you could seduce me into revealing everything with a Flat White coffee? Nice try though."

"What a weird way of putting that. Here I am, thinking we were having a lovely cup of coffee together, and all the while you're thinking I'm trying to seduce you." He gripped the small espresso cup handle between his finger and thumb and downed the remaining liquid. "If that was the case, we'd be in a bar."

They both grinned. By spicing the conversation up a little she had achieved a closer connection with him. She knew it, he appreciated it. Men can be put on the back foot when women introduce sexual connotations into conversations, but he had lapped it up. Far from backfooting him, he seemed to relax more. They finished their drinks and he waved at the coffee shop owner, who gave him an exaggerated wink that made her resemble Popeye. He spun his head round, but thankfully Eloise was not looking. What is occurring with these women, it's all about sex. As they stood up, he gave Val an admonishing shake of his head. They made their way out onto the street and headed off to collect some lunch. He looked through the window to see Val giving him a double thumbs up.

CHAPTER 11.

Come up trumps;
To complete something well or successfully.
The word trump in this context is a corruption of triumph, *which was the name of a card game, similar to whist, that was played in the 17th century. In triumph, as in whist, the trump suit was selected at random by the 'cutting' of the deck. Trump cards temporarily outranked other cards. Selecting the right suit to match one's hand was an advantage in the game and so* turning up trumps *became synonymous with success.*

Back at the station, the desk sergeant was in waiting for them as he wanted an urgent word with his DCI. Graeme sighed and rolled his eyes upwards as he asked Eloise to take a seat in the waiting area whilst he found out what it was all about. The issue that was vexing Sergeant Ross Piper so much, was where was he to put her until they heard from Supt Day? The interview room was needed, so it was a cell or an office upstairs. Graeme King reminded the sergeant that right now she was sitting in a waiting room and could be gone by the time they resolved this matter.

"Come on Ross, find somewhere, quiet, but where you can keep an eye on her."
"Shall I rustle up some potpourri. How about a HD TV with satellite?"
"Ross, I'm impressed. You know about potpourri. Leave it with me."
Getting into an argument was only going to waste time he did not have. DCI King collected Eloise and explained how he just needed to find a place for her until he knew how to proceed.
"If it causes too much of a problem, I'm quite happy to go home and come back tomorrow."
"I'd rather you stay at the station if you don't mind."
"As long as I'm gone by 3.30pm."

"Gone! Until I know how to proceed, I can't let you leave."

"Why? Am I under arrest?"

"No."

"Am I to be charged with an offence?"

"I don't know yet."

"But I haven't been as of yet, so on what grounds are you considering holding me?"

"If needs be I will charge you."

"For what?"

"Suspicion of murder."

"Graeme, by now I thought you would know I do my homework. My legal team, who are waiting in the wings by the way, would tear that to pieces, sue your constabulary for any number of reasons and you would get your backside kicked."

He was taken aback. All sweetness and light and then suddenly a sharp jab to the solar plexus. This lady was used to getting her own way and clearly did not like the chance of that not happening.

"Am I missing something here? You came to us. You have indicated you might be involved in a suspicious death. Yet, with all that going on, you want to go about your normal business? Oh, and let's not forget, that is whilst you're telling me you could put several million lives at risk. It is not every day we let potential mass murderers wander about our streets, so why should we you?"

"Those lives are at just the same amount of risk whether I am sat at home or in a cell. The one thing I'm sure we can agree on is that I am not your regular mass murderer. I am not looking for new victims; I can choose from five million for crying out loud. All of which means, there is no more risk by letting me come and go."

He breathed loudly. A sharp intake through the nostrils, followed by a controlled expulsion of used air through pursed lips. Then he picked up on something she had said, which had bypassed him first time round.

"Why 3.30pm?"

That question unsettled her, he saw it. In fact, was that some kind of tender spot she was protecting? It was as close to any display of a weakness as he had seen up to this point. Eloise knew it too. She had revealed a chink in her, up to that point, impregnable suit of armour. Damn. Fancy getting caught out by a simple query like that. As long as her family were reasonably distanced, cushioned, from the reverberations of what she was doing, she could be strong. No. She would be strong.

"As much as I humanly possibly can, I will keep things normal for my son. He is at 6th form and I do not want to distract him from his studies, so I will give you my days, but I want to be there for him in the evenings. I am not stupid enough to think he won't be distracted as this progresses, but the longer I can delay that the better."

DCI King processed all that information. Was she delusional, super smart or just mentally impaired by grief? Whatever it was, he felt like his 'kahunas were about to get slammed in a drawer', a phrase he had lifted from a former colleague of his. Her latest revelation had made it even more difficult for him to see how he could navigate a good path through this thick forest, laden with snares?

The immediate task was to find somewhere for her whilst he waited for Supt Day to call back. He led her upstairs. As they entered the open plan area, all eyes turned on the boss and this smart lady, who clearly Tim or Rebecca, or both, had spread the word on. There were two briefing rooms and he headed for the smaller of them. DCI King grabbed a chair and placed it just outside the door and offered it to Eloise. Catching Tim's eye, he beckoned him over. The walls had various case details on them, as did a large whiteboard, and before a member of the public could be allowed in, he needed to make sure data protection was being enforced and no sensitive details could be leaked.

Tim was made aware Eloise would be located in the briefing room and that it had to be cleared of all information relating to any cases. They began boxing up documents, taking down photo's, maps and diagrams. Using Tim's phone, they took pictures of the whiteboard, before wiping it clean. DCI King was going to use his phone to capture the whiteboards, but when DS Harrison asked how long it would take to get the snaps developed, he sneered, but accepted his phone was something of a collector's piece. He had been offered a smart phone, but when all you need to do is phone or text, why bother?

They were just about finished when Supt Day called. Graeme King left Tim to tidy the final bits up, told Eloise it wouldn't be long as he passed her and headed for his office. He closed the door.

"Hello Sir."

"You want to speak to me and it's urgent I understand."

"Yes Sir. Here's the shortened version. Eloise Langley is at the station."

"THE Eloise Langley?"

"One and the same. She wanted to discuss a suspicious death, went on to say she might be involved and that roughly 5 million other people could suffer a similar fate if we do not play ball."

"Have you charged her with anything?"

"No. That is where I need some guidance. If we attempt to detain her, those 5 million lives come into play. Right now, she is sat in my small briefing room, eating a meal deal and free to go whenever she likes. I have not formally interviewed her, because then we are on the road to charge or arrest, quite probably, and with the money she has behind her we could soon find ourselves neck deep in the smelly stuff."

"We can't be held hostage, you know that. Do we even know what she wants?"

"She won't tell me, until we've done some digging about the suspicious death she came in about. One more thing Sir. She offered to phone the Secretary of State for

Health, as she felt he might get The Home Secretary involved."

"Jesus H Christ!"

"Well, she didn't mention him, but I wouldn't put it past her. Now you'll understand why I'm kid gloving this all the way. I almost forgot, she wants to be leaving here by 3.30pm, so she can be home for her son, when he gets back from 6th form."

"Are you taking the mickey? You had not better be winding me up."

"Sir, be my guest, come and interview Mrs Langley if you need confirmation."

"Alright, alright. Exactly how does she intend to carry out this murdering spree?"

"Chipsules. I do not have all the details, but in essence, here is what she said."

DCI King briefed his Superintendent on how the Chipsules could be used to poison the body they were being carried in. Both men had friends and/or family this could affect and they soon realised that was the same for people up and down the nation. If this got out there would be pandemonium as everyone would want the implants taken out and the NHS could not cope with that level of activity. Plus, of course, if this woman was serious in her threats and she found out a mass removal of Chipsules was taking place, she might have the ability to take a few people out to deter any more such activity.

The conversation concluded with Supt Day demanding the result of their enquiries on Harry Vaughen's death within the hour. That would be 2pm and they had to make a decision then on how to proceed. Pompous, jumped up, little prick, thought Graeme King. There was no way he was going to get anything in that time and the Super knew it only too well. The purpose of saying it was so he could call The Chief and state what he personally had done. All that rear end covering and politics was not to DCI King's liking, but he had been given an order by a senior officer, so what could he do? Nothing, that's what. He could shout and scream, but that was not going to speed anything up, so best let his team get on with it free from any histrionics. He did the most sensible thing he could think of at that precise moment. He ripped open his cheese and onion crisp bag and savoured the taste sensation. No good for me they say; well, doing me a power of good right now. He unwrapped the BLT and then opened the sandwich in front of him, before placing several crisps on the contents. Not much beats a BLT with a crunch of cheese and onion. Simple pleasures, for a simple man and through a sarnie, a moment of release and refuge.

* * *

Superintendent Jeremy Day was back on the phone at 1.58pm, asking for an update. Nothing further to report. As Graeme had surmised, the Chief was now appraised of the situation and apparently even he was torn on the correct way to proceed. True to form Supt Day was playing it by the book. Demand an update from the detective leading the case; tick. Inform senior officer of case; tick. Graeme wondered how many ticks had been completed in the short space since they last talked.

If the Chief was not sure on what to do, that meant the case was likely to be moving out of the police enforcement remit and into politics. The police would still be doing the donkey work, but the guidance would come from the policing ministerial hierarchy. Instead of the customary carrot, there would be a truncheon and whichever direction this went, someone was in for a beating from it.

The outcome of this second call was, they agreed a further 'informal' discussion should take place between Mrs Langley and DCI King. The brief was to ascertain what she wanted from all of this, establish how she could follow through on her threats, if it came to that, and to get a gut feeling on how credible she was. Graeme swilled the remainder of his Diet Cola in its tin and then swallowed it in one big gulp. Wait for the burp, piece of chewing gum for the breath and then he would be nourished, ready for round 2.

CHAPTER 12.

Passing the buck;
Passing on responsibility.
Originated from a ritual practiced during card games. Card players used to place a marker, called a "buck", in front of the person who was the dealer. That marker was passed to the next player along with the responsibility of dealing.

Graeme King asked DI Blades to sit in again. If anyone thought he chose her for gender equality reasons, they were wrong. She was the best DI he knew. Smart, professional, asked the right question, in the right way, mostly at the right time and was like a dog with a bone once she was onto something. She just happened to also be a woman. The natural feminine qualities, of empathy and sensitivity, did help on many occasions, but that was an aside. He required the best person for this interview. Unquestionably in his mind, Rebecca Blades was it.
Eloise smiled as they entered the briefing room. She confirmed she was happy with the room being used for the 'chat'. Equally happy for it to be recorded on DI Blades phone, through the voice memo facility. She would do the same thing using her higher tech gadget. Eloise enquired if they had any news on Harry's passing and seemed disappointed, they had not yet managed to view any medical records, speak to his local surgery or contact his family. DCI King explained the difficulties in gaining such information in a short period of time and that the conversation with the family would be difficult; *We don't want to alarm you, but Harry may not have died of natural causes….* was going to need careful handling. She appreciated the complications and expressed genuine concern that the family should not be unduly upset any more than they already were. Graeme and Rebecca were like minded as she uttered this. A furtive glance between them confirmed it. The leap from menacing murderer to concerned individual was so at odds with each other and yet she negotiated the shift in stance with ease. Was she acting one, and if so which part?

Was there evidence of a split personality? Was she even aware of the mixed responses she was giving?

"It's difficult, Graeme. I'm hoping you, by you I mean the police of course, may spot something that indicates I can deliver on what I've said, but I hadn't really thought through all the consequences for the family. If you need more proof, then there is only one real way to do that. More casualties means more hurt for people, for families, just to prove a point. Slice it any way you want, that doesn't seem right."

"Can you activate these chips so they kill from within here?"

"Yes. Bit pointless me coming in and giving myself up if not."

"How? I'm intrigued."

"I am not going to divulge all my secrets, but for arguments sake, how about if the poison is already in the Chipsules? That could be released at given times over the coming days, weeks and months. Perhaps, just perhaps, it's already programmed in."

"So, if you don't do anything to trigger them, why shouldn't we just lock you up right now?"

"Do you know which people are affected? Are all the implants carrying poison or just some? Have I targeted certain people, classes, occupations, over others? I can prevent the release. Can you, without me?"

"How many of the 5 million are at risk?"

"Anywhere, between zero and 5.3 million and growing."

"Eloise, can you please tell me what it is you want?"

"Graeme, I like you and I knew there was a fair chance you would become involved if I used this police station, but I'm afraid you do not have the authority to grant what I want. No offence intended. So, if it's OK with you I will make a call and move things along a little."

Feeling dismissed, Graeme and Rebecca left the room and headed for his office. They reflected on the brief they had been given. Did they know what she wanted? No, but the call she was about to make looked likely to provide the answer to that in the very near future. Could she follow through on her threats? Seemed as if it was more about stopping what was already in place, so that was a yes. Gut feeling, was she credible? A unanimous affirmative to that one.

They could view the briefing room across the open area and she was walking about now, talking, using headphones. They became aware of DS Harrison putting his phone down and staring at them. He got up and headed their way, knocked and then entered.

"Boss, nothing yet from the medical people, but one of the local coppers knew the Vaughen family and has made some discreet enquiries with them."

"Oh no, I shudder when I hear 'discreet'..." DI Blades knew from experience how lacking in subtlety many uniformed officers could be.

"No, it's alright. Nothing to worry about. Anyway, Harry Vaughen's symptoms did change in the days leading up to his death."

"Like how?"

"He lacked energy, no real appetite, breathing problems, was becoming confused about simple things and almost as if his system was slowly closing down. I've looked them up and any of them could indicate poisoning."

* * *

Eloise had rung Barraclough, the Health Secretary's aide, as that was the number given her to contact that department. Turns out his name was Andrew. She explained she wanted to speak to John Kuria as soon as possible. Yes, it was very urgent. No, she couldn't give him any more details. He would see what he could do. He took her number and once again she emphasised the urgent nature; lives could be at risk. He understood. She rung off, but carried on pacing the room.

The phone rang, and it was Andrew Barraclough, "I'll put you through now. The Secretary has a meeting in 7 minutes, so I will be calling him for that in 5. OK?" She said she understood and then the line went quiet for a second.

"Eloise, lovely to hear from you and sorry, but this will have to be brief."

"John, thank you for making me a window to speak to you, I know how busy you will be. In a nutshell, I am in my local police station. I have provided some information on a suspicious death that I might be party to and I have some dema........., sorry, requirements, in relation to gaining justice for the murder of my son. If they are not met several other lives could be at risk."

She could hear breathing, but he took his time to respond.

"That is quite a nutshell. To help my understanding, when you say other lives could be at risk........"

"I have provided details of a death that might be the result of contamination from one of our Chipsules and if I can do that once, are you prepared to gamble on me not being able to repeat that feat?"

"I see. What scale are we talking here?"

"Millions. Millions of voters, John."

"Millions! Why exactly are you doing this? I know you said about justice, but what does that mean?"

"I probably don't have enough of your time to fully explain the justice I seek and I have a more urgent use of your time. None of this is negotiable, please let me make that very clear. I will not be denied my freedom to carry on my life as it is. I will be leaving this station at 3.30pm and if you attempt to have me stopped from doing that, on your head be the lives of innocent people. I will report to DCI King every day, but I refuse to be charged or arrested if that means I will be detained."

"You know full well I cannot agree to that."

"Perhaps not, but the Home Secretary certainly can. Once that has been agreed I will discuss the rest of my requirements with her. I think that's all for now, because with all due respect, there is little point in me discussing anything more with someone who cannot deliver what I need. Oh John, to be clear, I will be leaving here this afternoon and you might want to make The Home Secretary aware of that fact."

The next set of people were waiting to see the Health Secretary when he came off the phone, it was some senior executives from a private healthcare company who wanted to discuss commissioning plans for the NHS and how they could get involved. John Kuria instructed Andrew Barraclough to arrange a phone call with, Joy Hamilton, The Home Secretary for 30 minutes time and no jumped up civil service jobsworth was to get in the way; that call HAD to happen. He also wanted to know the Prime Ministers diary for the rest of the day. John Kuria welcomed the executives in and apologised, but the meeting would now only be for 30 minutes, as opposed to the 45 minutes they had planned. It might as well have been for 2 minutes, as the focus of his attention was elsewhere.

Andrew had done well. Despite his colleague at the Home Office being very much senior to him, he had used considerable influencing skills and made sure his boss could speak to the Home Secretary. A little bit of strong arm tactics using the name of his boss had oiled the wheels considerably too. John got Joy up to speed on the conversation with Eloise and made it clear that the first thing to decide was whether to detain her or not. Let a potential murderer, and possible mass murderer, walk the streets or prevent her from leaving and then who knows how many lives could be affected. Some choice.

Joy Hamilton knew how the police work, both formally and the often more effective informal approaches. Her dad had been a police sergeant, with 34 years' service. Whilst they might disagree strongly over how policing was resourced and managed, it was the proudest day of his life when she became Home Secretary. Anything she wanted to know about the way things get done in a police force, he was only too pleased to tell her. With no little relief, John Kurnia was rather pleased when his cabinet colleague said she would take it from here. He would email her over the PMs diary.

She called her permanent secretary in. Their discussion could have been lifted from a political farce.

"Clear my diary please."

"Secretary, we cannot do that, people are waiting for you and there are matters of state that need your urgent attention."

"Unless you clear my diary, millions of people's lives are at risk."

"I'll get onto it now……"

In this real life situation there was no laughing.

John Kurnia had mentioned a name of the DCI, Eloise Langley had been speaking to, she wanted to speak to him. A few civil servants were summoned to her room and given specific jobs and made only too aware of the urgency and importance of their task. One was to find out the line of command for DCI Graeme King. Another was to arrange a conference call with the minister for police, her special adviser on all things policing and the Chief Constable for the region where Eloise was at. Today, yes, it had to be today.

Graeme King was pondering what would happen at 3.30pm when his phone rang. The way he answered it did little to hide his agitation.

"DCI King, but this had better be mega important as I'm dealing with something very delicate."

"Good afternoon DCI King, this is the office of the Home Secretary. Please stay on the line." He was not conscious of the background music as he sat upright. Talk about squeaky bum time.

"Hello, this is Joy Hamilton. Is that DCI King?"

"It is ma'am."

"Oh bugger all that, can we stick to first names please? I'm Joy, and you are…"

"Graeme."

"Within the next few hours your line of command will know I'm dealing directly with you and to keep their noses out. Hopefully, you can relax a little now."

"Thank you for that, but with the greatest of respect discussing a case with the Home Secretary is not that relaxing."

"Do your best. My old man was a copper, so I'm on your side and by getting your guvnors off your back I thought you could open up a little better. By the way, feel free to say it as it is. I have zero tolerance for pratting about. No airs and graces, I prefer it straight and true."

Graeme gave Joy a full overview of the day so far and once again stated he was getting nervous about what to do as 3.30pm approached. She listened, she took notes and every so often she asked him to pause, whilst she caught up. What she did not do is interrupt. The more he talked unbroken, the less he would think about who she was and then he would reveal everything, which was likely to include details he would miss out if she kept jumping in. At the end she went silent for a while, as she digested the contents of her notes.

"Graeme. If you were me, would you let her go or detain her? There is no right answer here, actually, probably, just wrong ones. Tell me your thoughts."

"I have spent quite a bit of time with this lady today and let's be clear, she is no psycho just waiting to blow someone away. In my view, no-one is at more risk by her being let out or stuck in here. I would let her go, on the agreement that we can have officers situated around her home; out of sight, so having no impact on her son, but she would know they were there. I'd grab her passport of course."

He could hear the scribbling of pen on paper.

"I agree. See if she'll go for that. Graeme, she needs to be back there first thing tomorrow though."

Joy informed Graeme of the impending conference call and asked if he would mind joining. There was no pressure on him to provide input, if he wanted to, he could of course, but mostly she wanted him on there so he was completely informed on all matters to do with the case.

* * *

Graeme King discussed with Eloise who he had been speaking to and what they were proposing. "Here's my passport, I thought you'd never ask for it." She winked at him. Crikey, she was still so cool about everything. "Can I suggest we arrange a video call or Skype or something with the Home Secretary for the morning? I feel that would be the best way for me to discuss my requirements."

CHAPTER 13.

The whole nine yards;
Everything, the whole lot.
During the Second World War, gunners were armed with an ammunition belt
which was 27 feet long. To use the whole belt on the enemy was to go the
whole nine yards.

Eloise was back at the station for 9am. Graeme collected her from reception and escorted her to the briefing room. The Home Secretary had graciously agreed to the request for a video conference and arrangements were being made for this to take place at 9.45am. Basically, a laptop was being put in the briefing room. Eloise wondered who had used the term 'graciously', because Rebecca Blades delivered it, but it felt forced. Far more like she was repeating an Andrew Barraclough expression. Although Joy Hamilton had said to relax, both DCI King and DI Blades were about to conduct an interview in front of their ultimate superior officer, bar the Prime Minister, and neither wanted to look like an idiot. Eloise had asked for the meeting, but who knows what form or direction it would go? This was not a time to be unprepared. They were busy checking notes and agreeing their line of questioning, if called upon, and doing whatever else they could to be fully set for whatever was thrown at them. Rule number one, watch each other's backs; if one stumbled the other picked the baton up.

Eloise was emitting total confidence, but she was also very prepared. Her bullet point notes were there as an aide memoire, but she had rehearsed this conversation many times in front of the mirror at home, so she pretty much knew it off by heart. She was old school enough to bring a notebook with her main points recorded in it, along with other details she might need, but modern enough to be using an iPad as her main source of support with the major bullet points she would cover. Both were on the table in front of her. The iPad was far more impressive for making presentations and this was going to be one hell of a show.

Graeme checked on her at 9.30am, popping his head in the door. It was his briefing room, but was starting to feel like her office, as he always knocked before entering. He wanted to make sure she was feeling OK. She was. Had he made sure everyone knew she would be taping the conversation? He had. As he began to leave, she said, "Good luck Graeme. I know this is a biggy for you, but I think I will shoulder most of the work." He gave a purposeful nod to acknowledge her thoughtfulness and left. One step away and he paused, as if he had turned to stone. He knocked and entered the room.

"Eloise, despite not even knowing what you want, you are a brave woman to risk the life you have. I do not see you as the killing type, it has to be said, so I hope you get some of the justice you're after and some inner peace with it."

"Graeme, that's very sweet. Thank you. Appearances can be deceptive, so I wouldn't underestimate what I'm capable of if I were you." She wagged a finger in his direction. The way it was delivered was quite playful, but the message it carried was anything but. "I'm not here for some of the justice, I want every ounce of it. Sadly, at peace is not something we will ever feel again."

A moment of intimacy bridged their respective roles in this scenario for just a second, before morphing into something more awkward as reality bludgeoned through. Eloise looked away, stroked her notepad with the tips of her fingers, and then back up at Graeme. He was stuck in time, not knowing if to move would seem rude or whether to just carry on standing there like a cretin, not saying anything. Eloise came to his rescue.

"Shouldn't you be getting into full battle dress or something?"

"Aha, yes. We start every interview with a haka now, hope you don't mind."

* * *

Bang on time the laptop came to life with an 'incoming call' message. DI Blades pressed the 'accept' button and on screen the Home Secretary appeared. A roll call was held. In the briefing room were DCI King, DI Blades and Mrs Eloise Langley. With the Home Secretary was her special adviser, Shaila Ali, and a junior civil servant, Toby Waring. Toby had clearly been asked to do the technical bits of making the call, and he was dismissed once his function was complete; politely, but firmly. His feeling of almost euphoria to be given a task for the 'big boss' of the department, was replaced with the descending speed of a free-falling sky diver as he realised he would not get to see all the action.

The brief of the special adviser included all things pertaining to law enforcement, hence her inclusion. The Home Secretary set some ground rules, although everyone probably preferred informal terms, due to the nature of what was being discussed that would not be appropriate. Police ranks, Mrs Langley and Home Secretary were to be used at all times. Also, whilst Miss Ali was there as a source of support and expertise, she would not do the talking. Joy's experience with these conference type calls, told her it was more efficient and effective in communication terms if fewer people were seeking air time. Ideally for her the call would be concluded in 10 minutes. Not because it wasn't important, but because she had created a hole for this, where one had previously not been. Not that it needed saying, but as people get wrapped up in their own topics, they might forget she did have some other 'important' matters going on. Needed or not, she reminded everyone of this point in case the ten minutes looked like running over. Nods of agreement all round. As had been her practice up to this point, Eloise thanked the Home Secretary for her time.

"Mrs Langley, I have been briefed by the Health Secretary and DCI King on this situation, so, even though there are more grey areas than black & white, I believe I have a decent grasp on where we're at. The purpose of this call is to establish a way forward as you've thrown laid down police procedures into a complete and utter quandary. You might be responsible for one death, you claim to have the sword of Damocles over millions more, and yet, you will not accept being detained and if you are, that sword could come into play. I hope to help my officers decide how to proceed and DCI King believes that might be helped by knowing what it is you want from handing yourself in and making these claims. By the way, I know you want justice for the death of your son, I just don't know what that means in any detail at all."

Eloise breathed in deeply, her chest and whole upper body rising slightly as she did so. Glancing briefly at her notes, she looked directly at the screen and began.

"A drunk, exceeding the speed limit when he struck my son, who was on a zebra crossing, gets away with murder, manslaughter, or whatever else you care to define it as, with a paltry sentence. Jonas Rafferty killed my son. Jonas Rafferty destroyed the life we knew as a family. His actions meant a life of great promise was left unfulfilled. The sentence was a disgrace. Unless, of course, you are a rich father and man of influence, who can bend and manipulate the system through money and acquaintances. My son is dead and buried and will never see the light of any day, ever again. But, his killer will, as a free man, and all too soon. My son was called Tobias."

She stopped, the sound of his name once again provoked her tears and cracked her voice. His image and then a film reel of his life flashing through her mind. God, she missed him so much. From now on she would use his name, as 'my son' was impersonal. Everyone needed to understand this was a person, not just a term.

"Mrs Langley, are you OK to continue?"

"Yes. Sorry."

The tears were trickling down her face, slowing then surging, as they made their way. The normal instinct is to wipe them, or dab them, but she left them alone and tasted the salt as they reached her lips. She coughed, swallowed and continued. She had been preparing for this and some stupid tears were not going to derail her.

"As a family, we have been let down by legal practices that are unjust, archaic and plain wrong. Money and club membership should not trump doing the right thing. I can afford the best lawyers, but I had faith in our process and didn't think I would need them. If I had done that, I would be playing the system in exactly the way I am now so furious at. The fact I can, has no relevance to all those less well off families coming up against the rich and being trampled on. People in authority have a duty to everyone, not just their mates, not just those they play golf with, not just those who pay them handsomely. I want justice for Tobias. I also want justice for every family who has suffered like we have."

She paused, picked up her iPad and quickly entered the passcode. She had no need of the tablet as a prompt, she already knew exactly what she was going to say. What she did need, was a minute to gather herself ready for the big reveal.

"Home Secretary, here is what I want. I want Jonas Rafferty to stand trial again. I am not concerned with whether the charge is murder or manslaughter. What I am concerned about is the sentence."

"Mrs Langley, forgive me, but under no circumstances can we predetermine the sentence. Anyway, that would totally fly in the face of your calls for fairness."

"I was not meaning the sentence in terms of what the outcome would be. I am referring to the maximum sentence the judge can impose."

"Mrs Langley, for either murder or manslaughter the maximum is the same, life imprisonment. Was that not your understanding?"

"Yes, I fully understand that. However, he did not stand trial under either of those crimes. The skullduggery behind the scenes meant we were cheated out of that. So, as the justice system has failed me, failed my family and failed Tobias, I am seeking justice on my terms."

Eloise knew how to hold an audience in suspense. She had stood on enough stages at conferences to understand how to squeeze every last drop of anticipation out of the assembly. She looked at DI Blades. Then she turned to DCI King. A final, pointless, glimpse at her tablet and then her head rose to look directly at the Home Secretary.

"I want Jonas Rafferty to stand trial with a possible sentence of capital punishment. He took the life of Tobias. He should stand trial with a similar fate on the line."

"Are you serious?"

"I hope that has never been in doubt. I want the death penalty brought back for this case."

Everyone on the call fell silent. Just taking in what had been said. The Home Secretary excused herself and pressed the mute button her end and then went off

49

camera to have a discussion with her special adviser. In the briefing room it was weird, odd, almost eerie as the three occupants sat in silence. The two police officers knew the recording was still taking place, so any ill thought out comments could come back to haunt them, and Eloise was quiet, seeking any clues as to how her bombshell had gone down. With a blank wall being all she could see on the screen, the clues were not forth coming. However, her glare did not cease.

The Home Secretary and her adviser did not waste any time on inconsequential matters, they went straight into clarifying the situation, considering options and the best way forward. The situation was, they were being faced with either authorising the use of the death penalty as a sentence possibility, for this one case, or face this lady being able to follow through on her threat to kill random people and in unknown numbers. To reinstate the death penalty would mean parliament voting, that alone would put this matter in the public domain, and anyway if they agreed to one case, how many more blackmail situations would they face? The alternative was no more palatable. What about if it was more than a bluff? It would be inconceivable if people began dying and the government of the day knew it could happen and let it unfold. Politically, that was untenable. As human beings it was unthinkable. Joy Hamilton was struggling to focus with all the potential fall out there could be from this.

Shaila, her special adviser, was not being overly helpful, mostly just stating the bleeding obvious. However, she did propose the only real option there was and one Joy knew she had to use; involve the Prime Minister. Joy picked up the phone, *Cancel my next meeting....... I DON'T CARE, just cancel it. Then get the PM for me. URGENTLY.*

Their job now was to offer a proposed way forward to the PM, but ahead of that they had three people sitting in a police station briefing room, staring at an empty screen, apart from a 'muted' indicator. Joy sat down in her chair and turned the volume back on.

"My apologies for the delay. As I am sure you will appreciate Mrs Langley, there is no easy solution to this, so I will need some time before I can decide how to proceed."

"Home Secretary, that is what I expected. For the recording, let me state that an option you will consider is to look into removing as many of the Chipsules as you can. The practicalities of that are ridiculous and anyway, I would strongly advise you against such an action. Also, DCI King and DI Blades need support as to what to do in terms of releasing or detaining me. Can you authorise last night's remedy for the foreseeable future please?"

"I will give due mindfulness for your first point. I will consider whether to detain or release you and get back to you."

"That's fine. Thank you. However, at 3.30pm if you have not communicated your decision, I will put these two fine officers in something of a predicament. To detain me, they will need to use physical force and if that is the case, who knows what might happen."

CHAPTER 14.

The cut of your jib;
One's general appearance and demeanour.
Originally used by pirates in the 17th century the expression refers to the
forward sail on most ships. The course and speed of a ship is determined by the
cut of the ships jib so saying that you like the cut of someone's jib is a way of
saying, I like the way you're heading.

The Prime Minister was a long established politician, having been in the Houses of Parliament for 14 years. He had held a variety of cabinet and ministerial positions, became leader of his party nearly three years ago and just over a year later took on the office of PM. The election victory was for a number of reasons. Many voters were apathetic to the incumbent government at that time as they had fallen short on a number of major manifesto promises. In addition, too many senior members of government had got embroiled in, or tainted by, numerous scandals. The elected members should be representative of the public they serve, apart from when it comes to having affairs or being a touch greedy with their allowances, it seems. With their opponents' defences in tatters, the opposition were able to land punch, after telling punch, until the result was an almost foregone conclusion. Of course, not all the naughty boys and girls were on the government benches, but the opposition campaign manager had spoken to his miscreants personally.

Your reputation as a philanderer is your concern, mine is getting this party into power. The best line I've heard about you, is that you prefer Velcro to a zip. Well, for the foreseeable future I would appreciate it if you could have a combination lock fitted. To be frank, if what you're seeing is not your wife's brassiere, then you can kiss goodbye to your career.

Why was it easier to keep MPs in line when seeking power?

Peter Manger had a good amount of respect across both sets of benches and annoyingly for the opposition he was carrying a large share of the voting public with him through his policies. He was a practical, no-nonsense type operator. Prior to entering politics, he had been an army officer and then found out what a real battle is when he entered industry. It was easy to see him as the favourite uncle type, as his image was of a man who liked to smile, was confident and you could feel comfortable with. Fall into that trap when on the hustings or opposite him in the House and you were in trouble. He could be ruthless, exploited any chink in an argument and his wit was rapier like. Try to take him on in a battle of the put downs and you were on a loser.

He could not believe how rapidly his hair had greyed since he took on the top job. Understandable though, as the work was relentless. He had to be on top of every department brief, whilst looking for ways to improve the lives of every citizen, but do so without spending. The amount of money the country owed was colossal. So huge, that to anyone other than an anorak of an economist, it was unimaginable. He had shackled himself quite a bit on public spending by signing off on the manifesto he stood for power under. It declared, reducing the amount the government borrowed to zero over the term of the parliament as a priority. He could not accomplish that objective by allowing spending to get out of an exceedingly tight grip on the purse strings.

Once in power it soon became clear that meeting the manifesto pledge was unlikely, to put it mildly, so it was about making as much in roads as possible. He did not like breaking his word, but if he had admitted defeat straight away, he would have been accused of lying to gain the election win. The onset of his silver mane could largely be placed at the door of creating less of a need for money to be spent on defence, health, education etc., whilst fully aware to avoid much more creaking and straining at the seams they should invest heavily in those same areas. To remain popular, his government needed to do so without asking for more tax.

On his wall hung a quote by Groucho Marx;

Politics is the art of looking for trouble, finding it everywhere, diagnosing it incorrectly and applying the wrong remedies.

When appointing his cabinet, he made a point of directing them to read this quote. Most smiled. It was good they enjoyed it. Then he cautioned them; it was when they were angry or frustrated, they should remember it.

His phone call with the Head of the CBI had ended sooner than he expected, so he looked at his list of other calls to make and the one concerning the Home Secretary stuck out. It was not only urgent, but it was unlike Joy to ask him to make contact like this. She had been the Shadow Home Secretary, done a brilliant job, and carried on in the same vein since he appointed her after the election. He liked her, he trusted her, and she was the epitome of a safe pair of hands. He picked up the phone and instructed the member of his support team who answered it, to get the Home Secretary for him.

After some brief pleasantries, the conversation turned to the matter in hand and Joy briefed her boss on Mrs Eloise Langley, her history, her threats and her demands. Whilst no government can give into blackmail, the alternatives seemed equally troubling. This was not a bomb threat or a plane hi-jacking; they could be contained or eliminated. This was not a terrorist, in the way most people would think of them, holding the country to ransom for money or political reasons. This was someone who had made a massive contribution to the lives and wellbeing of thousands of people the length and breadth of the land. Many would know of her from TV as well, so conveying her as a potential mass murderer in waiting was going to be met with much scepticism. If her plight ever came out many people would understand, probably agree, with her anger.

The murder weapon was already in place, over 5 million times, so undoing that was a logistical nightmare, certainly not a short term solution and she was not going to give them the time to organise the extraction of all those Chipsules. However, before the options were considered in any level of detail, they had to decide whether to detain her. The PM asked Joy for her opinion.

"I am not sure what we lose by letting her return home every night. The 'damage', if you like, is already in place. We have her passport and we have officers stationed around her house. I know that we could be accused of giving in to her demands, but I would rather do that than risk a life. Her weapon of choice is not at her home or any location she can easily get to."

"So, I take it your view is to release her and then she attends for interview every day?"

"Yes, but we are not interviewing her as we would do normally. The DCI, a guy called Graeme King, has quite rightly said that if he does that, laid down procedure could require him to detain her, be that through a charge or an arrest. Do that and we ask her to show her hand and I'm not sure we want that. Certainly not yet, until we look into things a bit more."

"So, you not only want her to be able to go home every night, but you want freedom for your officers to interview her without having to follow police procedures?"

"Peter, based on the number of lives this could involve, I need to know if we will meet her demands. If not, then I will tell DCI King to carry on as he would for any other potential crime. If there is even a slither of a chance we will bend to meet her, then yes, I would seek your agreement to follow a new path. If that means, cabinet approval or sign off in the House or both, so be it. I will make the decision, but the graveness of what could happen means I would want your support for any such action."

"We have known each other for a long time Joy and based on what I know about you and your principles, are you really even suggesting we contemplate being held to ransom in this way?"

"No........but, I sort of get the feeling she has more to hit us with yet. I am exercising extreme caution in my every move. Thanks Peter, I will contact DCI King and tell him to follow procedure and that will take us wherever it does."

"Joy, you have always had a good nose for sniffing out trouble, so keep me close to this one please."

CHAPTER 15.

Go haywire;
To go wrong, to become overly excited or deranged.
Hay-wire is the light wire that was used in baling machines to tie up bales of
hay. At the turn of the 20th century the expression 'a haywire outfit' began to
be used. This was used to describe companies that patched-up faulty
machinery using such wire, rather than making proper long-term fixes.

DCI King took the call from the Home Secretary in his office. Up until now, he had never had the slightest contact or encounter with any high ranking politician and now it was becoming a daily occurrence. He let out a one syllable 'ha' of a laugh, as he recalled the moment he told his missus of who he had been conversing with. She had been most impressed. Another chuckle at the thought of her scolding him when he said he hadn't thought to tart up his appearance for this high profile meeting. As it happened, he was hardly the centre of attention, but she was right, he needed a haircut and the shoes could do with a polish. When the heck would he get the chance to visit the barbers until all this blew over?

He listened as Joy Hamilton recounted her discussion with the Prime Minister and went on to discuss how he was to proceed. Graeme King had sailed under the radar for all his career and now, almost overnight, he was a 'ping' on two of the most important politicians in the land. He knew that people would tell him this could make a career, but he also knew one false move and it could be a career breaker. Cover your backside, keep very alert and for anything controversial or unusual, seek guidance was what he kept telling himself. Senior people do not get that way by being left holding the baby. They know how to minimise their complicity and apportion blame, so he would watch out every step of the way.

The outcome of the call was that he should interview Mrs Langley formally and charge, arrest or release depending on what came out of the discussion. If that meant she was detained, then he was to play it by the book. He should inform

Superintendent Day of what was happening, but she would prefer if he kept the reins on the case. Mrs Langley seemed to like him and the connection they had made could prove useful further down the line. Did he have any questions? No. She gave him her Home Office email address and a mobile number. The email was for updates, the mobile number for advice or if he felt she needed to know something urgently. She wished him good luck and hung up. He hurled his body backwards, deep into the padding of the chair, to release his mind from the pressure of the call. He rubbed his face with his palms, slowly, and then much quicker. As his hands came to a standstill, his eyes were protruding over the top of his fingers. He closed them for a second. As soon as he opened them again, he slapped his cheeks and was up out of his chair. Back to business Graeme.

He knocked, Eloise waved him into the briefing room. They were the only two people in the room. He explained what would happen and said they would use one of the interview rooms for the formal discussion. She made two comments. Number one; that's expected, but a shame. However, she was confident it would soon be overturned and her demands acquiesced to. Secondly, she was leaving at 3.30pm and if he, or anybody else for that matter, wanted her to stay beyond that time, they would need to be ready to restrain her. He mentally noted, this was not the first time she had mentioned that. Was it so important to her to leave or was she teasing them into bodily preventing her from leaving for her own purposes? Both agreed to crack on. He would collect her in 30 minutes, she could have a toilet break in the meantime and she could organise a solicitor or lawyer if she wanted to.

DCI King called DI Blades into his room for a briefing as he wanted her to continue to interview with him. They were about 15 minutes into their discussion when he noticed Eloise had stuck her head out of the briefing room and was waving at him. He mumbled something like *Now what?* and headed to the briefing room. DI Blades followed him, but Eloise expressed her reluctance to continue if both officers were to be present. In the first instance it might be better if only DCI King was party to what she had to say. Who he chose to tell was up to him. A pensive stroking of his chin communicated he was mulling it over.

A nod of the head towards the exit and a look that very clearly said, *not now,* affirmed his agreement. He closed the door on an unimpressed Rebecca Blades. She had not said a word, but her whole demeanour was screaming 'huh'. The glance at Eloise, the scorching stare at him and a pronounced about turn, any soldier would have been pleased with, were not hiding her feelings at being excluded in this way. He could see her annoyance, so with both hands at about waist level, he motioned his palms up and down, ever so slightly, as the sign to ask her to remain calm.

"Eloise, has something happened?"

"Yes. Graeme, I am about to share with you some information that is sensitive and will have political ramifications. I presume you have access to the Home Secretary should something drastic happen, so I think it only fair to give you the choice to hand it over to someone more senior or hear it yourself."

"Christ Eloise, it's never a dull moment with you is it? Before I decide, can you give me any indication of the nature of the information?"

"Yes. At least one person has abused their position, using information that could only have come from what I have discussed in this police station."

"Abused! How?"

"Decision time Graeme. Do I tell you or the Home Secretary?"

"Me. Tell me."

"If you're sure."

She was seeking confirmation, before proceeding. He had the ear of the Home Secretary, but he could not abuse that and be calling her every two minutes. What advice would he give a colleague in a similar situation? He knew full well what he would say; grow a pair.

"Yes, you can divulge whatever it is to me."

"OK then. I can tell you that at least one person has had their Chipsule removed and that of their family members who were carrying the implant."

She stopped speaking. Was that it?

"Excuse my ignorance, but I don't do politics, I do law enforcement. It doesn't sound an unreasonable action from my point of view, so why are you telling me this."

She looked surprised. Might even be a trace of disappointment truth be told. In a deliberate tone, verging on deprecating, she continued.

"If a minister in a business related department, used information he found out through his political role to make money on the stock market, it would be called insider trading and he or she would be in serious trouble. The person I am talking about had access to confidential information, through their role as an officer of this government, and used it to their own benefit. They did so knowing full well what they did was not an option for the majority of the public."

Ah, the penny dropped. He might not be a politician, but he could see the potential scandal if what she was saying was true. The papers would be all over it, it would most probably be the headline story on the TV news and someone's career was over. He felt hot all of a sudden. Talk about a stressful situation. Focus man. What else do you need to know before contacting the Home Secretary?

"I need to know how you can be sure of what you are alleging."

"Before I tell you that, let me show you what I am saying is true. I have access to the data of every Chipsule in operation. If they no longer function, which includes being removed, the system we use informs our central computer and a warning is generated. We can then check if the removal was carried out for medical reasons with local health authorities, surgeries or whatever. I have my own, standalone, access to that same information, just in case someone on your side suggests turning

off our mainframe as a way of blocking me. I hope I don't have to remind you, that
to do so would carry unmentionable risks of course. Two days ago, Mrs Hilary
Vincent had her Chipsule removed. She lives at No 76, Andover Street, Colchester.
Here is her home telephone number." She passed him a slip of paper. "Please check
out what I am saying is true and then, when I reveal the name of the individual who
has used their position inappropriately, people will be readier to believe me."
Every time he thought he was making progress, Eloise threw in another curve ball. It
was as if he was wading through treacle again. He returned to his office and made
the call. He introduced himself and asked if he was speaking to Mrs Vincent. It was
her daughter. Understandably, she was very protective of her mother and would not
let her take the call until she knew a bit more about what he wanted, but could she
help? He explained it might not make any sense to Mrs Vincent as to why he was
phoning, but had she recently had her Chipsule removed. Yes, two days ago.
Unfortunately, she had been diagnosed with cancer and prescribed a course of
chemotherapy. Her consultant had said the way the drugs worked might not react
well with the implant so, until she was in remission, he suggested she had it
removed. Graeme King wished her mother well with the treatment, apologised
profusely for bothering them at such a difficult time and thanked her for the time
she had given him.
He headed straight back to Eloise.
"You were right about Mrs Vincent, spot on to the day."
"Graeme, I can be spot on to the minute it was deactivated if you like."
"I'm not sure exactly how, but your revelation will no doubt change things once
again, so I suggest we postpone the interview and I'll make a call to see how I play
things."
"Before you make the call, a couple of things that you might need to know. If she, I
presume your call is to The Home Secretary, wants more names I can provide them.
It will be pointless, and I hope it's becoming clear that I can deliver on what I say by
now, but if I need to jump through some more hoops to get that credibility, then I'm
happy to play along. For now, that is. Also, please don't waste some bright young
things time, by seeing if how I am informed about the deactivations can be turned
off. It can't. Remove the implants and I'll know, end of story, and I have already said
what will be the consequence of that. The name I have will shake the walls of No 10.
You have to make that clear to her, so she can decide who she wants me to relay it to.
One last thing, 3.30pm is looming......."
He left the briefing room immediately and as he got to his office door he shouted 'No
interruptions. None!' to the assembled staff. His door closed firmly, but without a
slam. Rebecca Blades had just begun to rise up to see if the interview was
proceeding. She plonked down again and petulantly threw her pen across the desk.

DCI King had expressly been given permission by the Home Secretary to call her. He had her mobile number and her email address to prove it. Without doubt, he was inner circle on this case and he had an absolute need to call her based on what Eloise had said. Yet, picking up the phone to speak to such a senior government official was not coming any more naturally to him. He made some notes, so he had a structure of sorts for when he called her and also, he thought, it was the best way of him not making a complete cretin of himself by missing something important out.

Arduously, the handset was removed from the cradle of his desk phone. It did not usually feel that heavy. He dialled the number; slowly, purposely. It rang three times before being answered. *Joy Hamilton, Home Secretary.* Graeme King introduced himself, apologised for needing to contact her and then went on to explain the purpose of his call. He had not gone ahead with the interview as he was unsure how this could affect things. He was not in the politics game, but he did know when something had all the hallmarks of a ticking bomb, politically speaking. Also, Eloise kept on prodding him about 3.30pm, so time was a factor too.

The Home Secretary told him to hang up and she would call his mobile in under 5 minutes. That would give her time to be somewhere private and him time to get to Eloise and be ready for her call. "No point faffing about, let's find out what she's got."

He was starting to wear the carpet tiles out between his office and the briefing room. Back he went, knocked and entered. He explained the Home Secretary would be calling very soon. His mobile ringtone of 'Time Passing' rang out, he thought it was very apt for his job, as they were always up against the clock for one reason or another. It was Joy Hamilton, she asked to be put on speaker and Graeme confirmed there was only him and Eloise in the room.

"Right Mrs Langley. The floor is yours."

"DCI King will have told you I know when my Chipsules are removed and that he has corroborated this with one such person from a name I gave him. I can provide as many as you like but be assured they will all check out as 100% accurate. However, the name I am about to give you will provide a further five instances for you to check, which I hope you will agree should be evidence enough. The five names are the person in question and four family members. A person of seniority has wilfully abused their power and position."

"I understand you believe these implant extractions have taken place off the back of your discussions over the past few days. How can you know that?"

"With absolute certainty, I cannot. However, based on the medical benefits of the Chipsules, they are rarely taken out and only with good reason. Good, medical reasons, I should add. I will be interested to hear of the reason of significance for five members of the same family to have them removed in such a short time span. Not only that, but the time span just happens to fit very nicely with my visit to the police station. Once this person is challenged, they either have a verifiable reason, or they abused their position. It's as simple and straightforward as that. We both know which one the odds are stacked on."

"Mrs Langley, please share with me who this person is."

"Home Secretary, this person can leave their job for whatever reason you care to communicate through official channels, with no scandal for your government to face. That is, as long as my demands are met. If not, every media outlet I can find will know what happened."

There was an almost palpable sense of annoyance coming out of the phone.

"Please do not keep threatening me."

"I'm not. It is not the word I would choose to use, but if that is what you call it, I'm 'threatening' the government, of which you are a part."

"Who is it?" The tone was sharp, short on patience.

"John Kuria. The Health Secretary."

The disclosing of that name caused a Doodlebug moment. They were bombs used to terrorise the inhabitants of London during the second world war. They made a lot of noise flying above until they ran out of fuel, at which point they dropped and exploded. There had been a lot of noise, but with that revelation the sound was achingly quiet. Both Eloise Langley and Joy Hamilton knew if that got out into the public domain they would not have to wait long for the explosion.

The Home Secretary was not the sort of person to be intimidated easily, if at all, but she did know when it was right to be concerned, afraid even. They were being totally outplayed by this woman. The job of the government is to protect the people they serve and yet, whilst they were being held ransom to the tune of all those lives, they were scoring own goals and emboldening their nemesis.

To those in the minority who master the use of silence, they can become better managers, presenters and interrogators, because so many people are uncomfortable with the void of no-one talking. Eloise was relishing this particular moment of hush, as it told her she had scored a bullseye. A senior official of the government and holder of one of the great offices of state was speechless. To have such a high-ranking person as the Health Secretary make a schoolboy error of this magnitude was priceless for her cause, because the only person who had the authority to determine on what happened now was the Prime Minister. She wanted him involved and at the earliest opportunity. If he could manage this at arm's length, he would be demanding containment, no negotiation, follow the regular procedures and be putting the squeeze on his ministers to resolve the matter, efficiently and quietly. Once she got him personally involved, it became more difficult to maintain such an aloof stance. What a present this was; the Prime Minister was coming to her party.

CHAPTER 16.

Fools rush in where angels fear to tread;
The rash or inexperienced will attempt things that wiser people are more
cautious of.
'Fool' is now a more derogatory insult than it was when this proverb was
coined, in the early 18th century. At that time a fool wasn't a simpleton,
lacking in intelligence, simply someone who had behaved foolishly. 'Fools rush
in...' has a precise derivation, in that it is a quotation from the English poet
Alexander Pope's An essay on criticism, *1709. The 'fools' that Pope targeted there*
were the literary critics of the day.

Joy Hamilton was split by her loyalties. Personally, she was friends with John Kuria and she considered him a good, competent MP and cabinet member. He was also a rising star of the party, considered a shoo-in for the top job at some point. If that transpired, future jobs for her might depend on the relationship she held with him. Having looked like a probability before this came about, all that could change. Then again, these things can blow over and John Kuria might come back stronger than ever. Who knows, he could be back almost as quickly as it seemed his impending departure would be. He was still a young man in government circles, so time was on his side. He was also fortunate enough to live in a more tolerant age than some of his predecessors, in that failures of some sort, sexual indiscretions and other examples of poor judgement, were no longer the fatal blow they once were to politicians. Professionally, she ought to talk to the Prime Minister. He should know first and decide what action to take. If anything had happened like this in her department she would have wanted to be informed instantly and definitely be the first to know. If the culprit had been tipped off, she would find who did that and have their guts for garters. That would be exactly the same if she were PM.
The pondering was soon over. She was a member of Her Majesty's government and she always had to do the right thing by the British public. She called the PM's private

office and requested a window be found for her to have a meeting with him today, as soon as possible. Joy didn't respond well to the *No chance* response she got.

"I am the Home Secretary. I have seen the PMs diary for today, so I know he is at No 10. I am leaving now and will be with you in under 30 minutes. You have a choice. Either get me a slot with the PM or explain to him tomorrow, why a scandal was not conveyed to him that could result in horrible press headlines, a cabinet reshuffle and more spinning than Torvill & Dean at their best. I suggest you get me my window."

DCI King had not been instructed what to do about Eloise, such was the impact of her naming and shaming. The Home Secretary was clearly taken aback by what she had been told and was soon leaving the call. There are times to cover your bum and times when you do not act like some pathetic needy person and ask questions you can deal with yourself. He told Eloise to go home. Same conditions as last night, he would keep her passport and officers would be in the vicinity of her home all night. Also, had she got his number in her contacts? Based on what he just heard he guessed his phone might ring a few times that evening, and he was happy for her to be in her own home as long as she would take his calls. Eloise agreed. If a more senior person countermanded his decision to let her stay at home overnight, he would call her in. With that came a caveat. Come freely or be marched in. He needed to organise the officers who would be on duty at her house and then she might as well leave and he would see her tomorrow morning.

"I don't suppose you know where I can get a suit of armour do you? Just planning ahead knowing you're back soon."

"No, afraid not. However, I imagine I know where there will be a job vacancy very soon."

"You knew that would happen didn't you?"

"A hunch. No matter how much power and status they have, these people are only human after all. Graeme, I must apologise for all the grief I'm causing you, but please understand how important this is for me. I am not out to make life difficult for you, but nothing will stop me from getting the justice Tobias deserves."

"I understand fully the importance of this to you and no-one can doubt your determination." He moved his head to one side, so his chin was pointing left, and he scrunched his mouth a little. His inner dialogue was being played out through his gesture. He probably should not say anything, but he wanted to, it was almost as if he was being compelled to. "Eloise, I have family with those Chipsules implanted in them. If I hadn't been so busy with all this going on, that call could have been about me."

"I hoped you would be involved in my investigation and that was for a very good reason. You're a good man and a good police officer. I'm not sure that thought would have been entertained by that principled brain of yours. One thing I know for certain; if you were the Health Secretary, with all the responsibilities and expectations on behaviour that come with the job, you would not be placing yourself ahead of the whole country. I promise you this, whatever happens to me your family are as safe as houses when it comes to those Chipsules. Listen carefully Graeme; DO NOT have them removed. Those you love are in no danger from them."

He was taken aback a bit by her statement. Once this all went public those would be words welcomed, sought even, by millions of people and many more million family members. He had never considered that his family would be treated any different to anybody else. The impact of what she had said would take time to process fully. "Thank you, that is a relief."

Graeme strolled the short route back to his office and announced to everyone in earshot, he would see DI Blades and then he was open for business. Suggestive comments and wolf whistles rained all around Rebecca Blades as she walked across the room. She grinned. If it had been one of the others, she would have joined in. Their job often involved dealing with serious and disturbing matters, so any chance to shine some light through the cloud of bleakness was taken eagerly. She loved the banter. One of her female colleagues was bent over the desk, bum in air, jiggling it suggestively. A male colleague asked if she needed to borrow any handcuffs. She reached the door to the office, grabbed the door and just before she closed it, an unpleasant hand signal was issued to her hecklers. As soon as it closed another derisory howl went up.

The two detectives grinned at each other. DCI King looked down, leaned forward and his demeanour became very stern. He was about to upset her big time. He knew that, because if it had been him, he sure as hell would have been.

"Rebecca, I'm sorry, but for the time being you can't be party to this investigation." He saw the displeasure rise through her features. Her eyes were instantaneously at boiling point. She went to speak, but he cut her off.

"Just hold on and I'll try to explain. Through that roaring temper of yours you might not hear me, but hopefully you will recall some of what I say later. I hope you'll agree I try to be as honest and open with you as I can, but I cannot share with you what I have just been told. Plus, Eloise is landing significant blows on some senior people right now. It seems an idiot, and an idiot who should know better, has used confidential information for their own purposes. That information was gained from within this station."

Rebecca Blades was respectful, but still her voice was not disguising her annoyance. "Are you taking me off this case and if so, why?"

"Let me answer both points. No, I'm not. Like it or lump it, you are going to have to trust me on this. I doubt very much I will have anything more to do with this investigation and I expect a call to confirm that any second now. However, and you listen good to what I am about to say, IF I am asked to carry on, I will ask for you to be involved and then I will fully brief you. That said, as it stands, I am completely in the dark about what will happen next."

He scoured her face for any sort of acknowledgement. No change. She gave nothing away.

"That's all, DI Blades. Thank you." He had zero tolerance of what he considered immature behaviour expressed in this manner. Let her cool and then see if they could talk sensibly. In the meantime, she was best out of his sight. She looked surprised at his dismissal of her. Rather than storm out, she got up very deliberately, opened the door, turned round, only to find him looking at some paperwork on his desk, and left. Part dismayed, part disgusted at his apparent lack of concern for her feelings, she strode back to her work station. Her daze was brought to an abrupt halt by someone carrying on the banter from where they left off when she had entered the office; *Have you been fully...de-briefed?* The tone of the 'not now' this generated and the stare that accompanied it, told everyone the joke was over.

DCI King answered his mobile phone, it was Joy Hamilton. Even though she knew there was no need to say it, officially she had to remind him not to breathe a word of what he had heard to anyone for the time being. He was a little irked that she felt the need to call him for that, but he reassured her he was sworn to secrecy on the matter. He told her he had decided to let Eloise go home again tonight. Joy took a moment to think about this. Damned if we do, damned if we don't. It was his call and she confirmed he had her support.

She told him what he needed to know. But no more. She was heading to see the PM and would let him know what happens from there. As it stands, the approach with Mrs Langley would be to carry on as he had been doing. She should come in, he was to make her comfortable in the briefing room and from there, who knows? He smiled at this last comment, he liked her style, her honesty.

"Home Secretary, by the way is that what you prefer me to call you or ma'am?"

"Ma'am! Yuk. When it's me and you it's Joy and Graeme, when anyone else is listening in it's Home Secretary and DCI King. That OK?"

"Perfect." A surprised tone in his voice. He was not expecting that level of informality.

"Graeme, I am putting a massive amount of faith, and a fair dollop of trust too, in you right now, so first names seems appropriate."

"Of course. What I was going to say is, how long can we keep this up? A decision needs to be made soon. Within the station, the gossip and rumours are gathering strength about why this woman can come and go as she does, but also the press will get wind of her being here soon. Whilst that's not particularly an issue for me, I'm guessing your advisers will have kittens trying to explain it."

"You're right. However, we have to balance making the right decision, with how long we take to make it. The PM will do the right thing. I hope we have news for you in the morning."

A couple of pleasantries later and the call ended. Heads were popping up and down like Meercats as he looked through his window. This was not the only case he was in charge of and he had team members waiting for him to get off the phone so they could brief him and agree what to do next. He got up, opened his office door wide. That was a sign he was available, and the race was on to get to him first.

CHAPTER 17.

Up to scratch;
Good enough to meet a particular standard.
A phrase used in pugilists' fights. A line was scratched on the ground to which
the contestants had to put their forward foot before the fight could begin.

Prime Ministers do not have free slots of time. Every minute of the day is allocated to meetings, briefings, phone calls or any other number of activities. Meals are always 'working' with either senior civil servants, cabinet colleagues, dignitaries or any other number of people who had been lucky enough to get in front of the top politician in the country. The height of personal free time was a visit to the loo, although it was well known some of the support team thought a catheter or commode would be more practical. If anything urgent comes up, someone or some thing is cancelled, delayed or has their time reduced. It's that simple. Once an appointment is made, it is protected with the ferocity of a Lioness with her cubs by the civil servants.

So when Peter Manger was informed his meeting with the Cabinet Secretary had been cut in time to allow him to see the Home Secretary, he knew it was nothing trivial. Joy Hamilton did not need her hand holding to run her department and if she was coming to see him face to face at short notice, it was of significant importance. As she entered his office, he could see by the look on her face that she was troubled.

"Peter, thank you for seeing me. I had to use my pointy elbows to get past your staff, but I had to do this face to face."

"What the hell is going on Joy?"

"We discussed Eloise Langley and I said rather than be held to ransom we would proceed by the book. Well, I need to once again check you want to continue in this way, as she has information that will damage the government, the party and in turn, no doubt you."

"For crying out loud, what next from this woman? OK, let's hear it."

"I am not finding this easy and I've been struggling with my conscience about the best way to deal with this, so just so you know the person this concerns is not aware I know what they've done. I wanted to tell them as a friend, but my professional loyalty is to you."

"No judging from me. What's happened?"

"A senior member of your government has used information they obtained through their political office for the benefit of their family. Eloise Langley knows and is threatening to put it in the public domain."

"Let's cut to the chase Joy. Who and what?"

"John Kuria. He has had the Chipsules removed from members of his family."

"He what?"

"Based on the information he gained from Eloise, he has already had the Chipsules removed. I understand it's the human, family man thing to do, but Peter, I don't need to tell you what the media will do to us if this gets out."

"Perhaps I have underestimated Mrs Langley and as such I hadn't really considered it until now, but the headlines, the interrogations, the character assassinations; yes, it will hurt us."

"Plus, the genie will be out of the bottle. 5 million people, and all their loved ones, will want assurances about their life expectancy or we will have mass demands for the Chipsules to be removed. We couldn't meet that demand and Eloise has already said, even if we could, we will begin putting those same lives in peril from her."

"How can she possibly know about John?"

"Apparently, she knows about each and every Chipsule. She proved it too."

"You've had time to think about this, so what would be your recommendation?"

"Peter, it is your decision, but I can't see how he can stay. Your clever little PR people will need to consider the best way for that to happen. Then, I think we call a cabinet meeting. I am coming to the decision that we might need to meet her demands. Politics aside, we are talking about the lives of millions of people here."

"Am I hearing you correctly? John will go, the details I'll sort with him. No other option. Then, you are telling me to call a cabinet meeting to discuss the possibility of bringing back the death penalty for a one-off situation, because this lady does not like the judge's decision at the first trial? Joy, you know that makes no sense."

"Peter, God forbid this happens, but if you were threatened by a nuclear bomb strike on one of our major cities, would you consider negotiation, compromise or would you just say we don't give in to terrorists?"

"Possibly, who knows? But we are not talking about a nuclear bomb."

"No, you're right, because that would kill hundreds of thousands. This is far more serious as we are talking about 10 or 20 nuclear bombs worth of human life taking."

"Do you believe she could do that?"

"No idea, but I'm not about to suggest we play chicken with her. I get the feeling she knew someone would use their position to have the Chipsules removed. She's ahead of us. She's playing with us"

"I need to think about this."

"I know you do. Peter, we have to make a decision soon. Politically and legally, she is taking the mickey out of us. How many days can this potential mass murderer turn up at the police station and then go home without being charged? Equally, we cannot lightly gamble with so many lives and she has said she will not wait forever. Thanks for your time, and Peter, sorry to land something like this on you."

Joy left the Prime Minister's office. He then called in Robert Moore, his private secretary. The instructions were;

Cancel the meeting with the Foreign Secretary and no interruptions for the next 30 minutes. Pencil in a provisional meeting with every member of the cabinet for 8am tomorrow morning. They were to clear their diaries; no exceptions, no excuses. He would confirm later today.

Get hold of John Kuria. He wanted to see him in person today.

His permanent secretary was to be back in 30 minutes with a complete list of all cabinet members, ministers and those names on the succession plan. A mini reshuffle was imminent.

Sometimes the job of a permanent secretary is to question. Sometimes their job is to just do. Today was not a day for questions. When it comes to managing your manager, reading body language is crucial and the message given off today was, DON'T ASK. Robert Moore did not. He left. Plenty of time to obtain a better understanding later on.

Peter Manger then picked up his personal mobile and called his wife.

"Hi.........just a quick call.........we talked about discussing with the family the possible dangers of the Chipsules......just put that on hold for now............."

CHAPTER 18.

Cold shoulder;
A display of coldness or indifference, intended to wound.
The origin of this expression is that visitors to a house who were welcome
were given a hot meal but those who weren't were offered only 'cold shoulder
of mutton'.

It was rare for a Prime Minister to have uninterrupted thinking time, but it was extremely rare to be dealing with a situation like this. The COBRA committee had been called to discuss terrorist actions which had, or could, affect the population, but this was different. Word on any minor or major terrorist activity was spread far and wide through social media and with 24 hour news it was reported, dissected, blame apportioned and solutions suggested to prevent further atrocities. All done in the blink of an eye. Experts were seemingly easy to find for these broadcasts, as were people who had an opinion, a loud voice and were not afraid to use it.

We are delighted to be joined by the Metropolitan Police Commander with responsibility for Anti-Terrorism and the broadcaster and celebrity show regular.......

Peter Manger found it laughable, but also recognised he might be able to top up his pension if he could get his name on whatever list these people were called from. No shortage of work for him on Radio and Breakfast TV shows. However, his mind was back on what was no laughing matter.

As with every decision he had to take, there were no right or wrong answers, as there is no crystal ball to show how they will pan out. Follow procedure and risk lives; how many, no-one seemed able to say. Alternatively, give in to the demands of one person and that opened the flood gates for any number of terrorist groups, or individuals with a cause, to attempt to hold HM government to ransom.

With so many lives at stake, this was not a decision for one person to take, irrespective of their position. He would call a meeting, but not under the banner of COBRA, even though Cabinet Office Briefing Room A would be used. When those meetings were called, it was often widely communicated and acted, in part at least, as a way of re-assuring members of the public that their government was on it and in control of the situation. On this occasion, confidentiality was of vital importance. Certainly, at least until decisions were made on how to contain the situation.

First things first. Who should attend? All cabinet members, obviously, plus senior ministers from the Health, Justice and Home Office departments. Inter-departmental co-operation was going to be vital for agreeing a cogent plan. The Metropolitan Police Commissioner. The Chiefs of Staff, as the military might well be needed on the streets for public order reinforcement or to support medical personnel. The heads of the military did look after the best part of 200,000 soldiers, sailors and airmen & airwomen too. Managing the fears of these people, whilst still protecting our shores from all the other bad people in the world was going to take careful planning, so the sooner they could consider the situation and formulate plans the better.

So far, easy and straight forward. Now it got more contentious. If he was to gain support for the decisions he would take, along with those in the meeting, he needed the approval and engagement of the other major political parties. Party rivalries are not important when matters like these need attention. He decided to speak to the leader of the opposition to personally invite her and provide a pre-brief. He would also invite the leaders of the ruling parties from the Scottish Parliament and the National Assemblies of Wales and Northern Ireland.

There was a knock on his door and in walked his permanent secretary with the lists as requested. Had 30 minutes flown that quickly? Indeed it had. He took the lists, gave them a quick once over and put them to one side. Peter Manger told his PS that he wanted the meeting, who to attend and that its convening was confidential for the time being. Unless they were hospitalised or out of the country and couldn't get back, he expected all the members of his government to attend. Everyone else could send a deputy, but the matter of national importance that was to be discussed should convince the senior officials to attend wherever possible. Apologise for the short notice and then make the arrangements.

It was time for questions. The PS coughed;

"Excuse my intrusion Prime Minister, but what the hell is going on?"

"I can't say too much right now, but all I will tell you is, I have never felt more out of control about making a decision than I do this one. For now, just make the arrangements please. Oh, first of all, can you get me the leader of the opposition on the phone?"

Robert Moore had been a senior civil servant for a substantial period of time and was unaccustomed to being kept out of the loop. It annoyed him. When politicians want the support of the bureaucracy, they were all sweetness and light. Yet, every so often they became so swept up with their own importance they forgot the likes of a private secretary would still be around long after a general election had seen off their incumbent boss. He knew more secrets than most, so what was the point of being so petty?

"As you wish, Prime Minister." His sullen, mildly histrionic exit was completely wasted as this incumbent boss was already on to the next job of the day.

Alone again, Peter Manger began to look through the lists as he turned his head to who would be the new Health Secretary and how the dominoes would fall from there. His phone rang, it was the leader of the opposition.

"Hello Phyllis............no, no snap election, ha ha......... nooooooooo definitely no sex scandal involving myself about to come out through any kiss and tell revelations. I'm surprised you wouldn't think I would be more careful. I'm afraid it's rather more serious than any of that. In short, someone is holding 5 million lives to ransom and wants us to bring back the death penalty for a one-off case." The jollity of the call up to this point was replaced with a hush. "You still there?........Well, if I didn't think it a credible threat, I doubt we would be discussing it. I'll give you as much detail as I can, but first of all can you make arrangements to be at Downing Street for 8am tomorrow?......Yeah, fine. Once you're sure, call me back. Oh, by the way. You'll be pleased to know this has caused me some political damage as one of my secretaries of state will be leaving their post forthwith....... Yeah, laugh it up while you can."

John Kuria knew it was serious and he knew it was not good news. A summons to call on the PM in person was not likely to be rosy. What could it be? Departmental fiscal cuts? Had the latest data been so bad that it warranted a face to face rollicking? No matter how hard he racked his brains, he could not come up with whatever it was.

He was no sooner in the front doors of Downing Street, than he was being shown into the PM's office. Now it was confirmed. This was really bad news.

"John, come in."

"Hello Peter."

"Sit down John, please."

"Smelly stuff hit the fan has it?"

"I'm afraid so. No point beating around the bush, it seems you have made an error of judgement."

"I have?"

"You were party to some conversations concerning Mrs Eloise Langley and have used that information for your personal benefit."

"Peter, am I missing something here?"

"I think you are missing the fact that Eloise has the ability to track each and every Chipsule implanted across the nation. That means when you and your family rapidly began having them removed, she knew."

"Oh, I see. I had no idea she could possibly know. I was protecting my family."

"Not that it helps much, but it appears she knew someone would do this. It was just a matter of who and when."

"What happens now?"

A puff of the cheeks from Peter Manger as he let out a large sigh. 'Sacking' people, as the press loved to call it, was never an easy task for him to carry out. John was a good secretary of state and had the wit, wisdom and personal wherewithal to strengthen any cabinet, so letting him go was difficult, However, keep him on and he was a liability. That meant his position was untenable. No point in letting him cling on and hope nothing came out. Better to be decisive and limit the lasting damage to all concerned, including the party.

"You step down as Health Secretary, citing ambiguous personal reasons, sit on the back benches for a while and then work your way back in. Although I have to tell you, if it does come out what you've done, your route back in will be very difficult."

"Peter, it's not that serious what I've done. Silly, yes, but serious enough to lose my job? Really?"

"The problem is, Eloise is likening your act to financial insider trading and that is how she will portray it to the media. If you try to hang on, you will get zero support from me, as you then affect my government. Fact is, if you attempt to fight my decision, in all likelihood you risk damaging your career beyond any hope of mending it."

"Are you saying in my shoes, you would not have considered doing exactly the same?"

"It makes no difference what I might have considered; you, followed through on it. John, you might have lost your job, but you might also have saved the lives of your family. I probably shouldn't say this, but keep some perspective here. Maintain a dignified silence, go back to being a brilliant MP and if this all goes away quickly, you could be sitting on the front benches in no time at all. John, I'm sorry. She rolled the dice and you got played."

CHAPTER 19.

Between a rock and a hard place;
In difficulty, faced with a choice between two unsatisfactory options.
During a dispute between copper mining companies and mineworkers, the
workers approached the company management with a list of demands for
better pay and conditions. They were refused. The mineworkers were faced
with a choice between harsh and underpaid work at the rock-face on the one
hand and unemployment and poverty on the other.

Peter Manger was at Cabinet Briefing Room A good and early. He wanted to run through his introduction, plus, and most importantly, check again the main body of what he intended to say. Sitting on one seat he placed some papers on the next chair to reserve it, as he wanted to make sure Joy Hamilton was alongside him. This meeting had been her suggestion, or at least she had sown the seeds, so he wanted a fully paid up supporter right by his side. Already this morning he had met with senior members of his staff, dealt with any pressing matters and given them clear guidance on what could and could not remain in his diary over the coming days. At any given point in time he might need a window to react to whatever this situation threw up, so a rammed to the rafter's catalogue of meetings was not going to be practical, let alone wise.

Close by him were a few junior members of his team buzzing round, organising drinks for the table and getting ready to greet the attendees as they arrived. Joy was first to join him and brought with her a coffee from Costa. "Thought you might need this." He smiled and raised the disposable cup in a cheers/thank you type salutation. Joy tried to read his face. There was always a deep concentration etched across his features as he prepared for any meeting like this, as he was not the sort of man who would want to show any weakness. He would want to know his brief inside out and upside down. The seven Ps, he used to tell all his new junior ministers; Proper Prior Planning Prevents Piss Poor Performance. It had two uses. Firstly, it made it clear that with all the media scrutiny on every letter of every word they would say, there was no excuse for not knowing their subject and reading widely around it. Secondly, if anyone turned their nose up at the use of the word 'piss', he might question their readiness, their mental toughness for the role of a senior politician. There was no place for everyone minding their Ps and Qs when discussing emotional and important topics around the table, that could impede the speed of progress and he was not having that. Being thin skinned had never struck him as a good trait for any politician.

Joy Hamilton noticed an extra edge about him today. Could it be the list of attendees, not all of whom were regulars at these gatherings, could it be the mini re-shuffle he had on his mind or was it the content of this briefing? She gently nudged his arm to get his attention. As he looked up, she conveyed her message in a quiet voice, but with her lips overworking each word.

"If at any point you need to gather your thoughts, just give me a look and I'll jump in to give you a break. I think we need to agree in advance it will probably be absolute tosh I come out with, so no judging me on that."

He smiled and responded in a vaguely furtive manner. "Thanks Joy. Do we need a signal? I mean if every time I look your way, you start babbling on utter rubbish, then I can't see that being helpful."

"No signal required Peter. I will be able to pick up on your profuse sweating and look of abject horror as my cue. Second thoughts, both of those are normal for you, so perhaps we do need a signal."

There was a dull tap as he clinked recyclable cups with her. It expressed his thanks for the needed diversion and to admit defeat in the joust. "Cow." He said under his breath as they withdrew the cups. "You are very welcome, Prime Minister."

The room was starting to fill now, so Peter rose and greeted everyone. Those he was more familiar with got a squeeze of the shoulder as he passed and a quick 'Hi' or 'Hello' as they looked up to see who it was. For those less familiar, he welcomed each and every one with a firm handshake and a few words. He always shook hands, no matter what the sex or culture of the person he was meeting, as it was one less thing to think about. He was a typical awkward Brit and by taking the lead with an outstretched hand he removed all that fuss. If they preferred a kiss on the cheek, or both cheeks, they would instigate, and he would respond. Royalty or Heads of State was different of course, and he would be briefed by some expert on how to receive them.

He certainly knew how to work a room. Everyone felt welcome, many were left smiling through some quip he had made and most of all he had the ability to energise the room. Joy got the final squeeze on her left shoulder as he returned to his seat and it lingered a little longer than it had on the others. He caught her eye, raised his eyebrows up high, held them for a second and then returned them to their natural resting place as if to say, 'Here we go'. Sitting firmly down, he slurped a bit more coffee, which had cooled considerably during his tour of the room, read through his opening line and then stood up. The act of sitting down and then standing up was how he would alert those present that proceedings were about to begin and they should come to order.

"Good morning. Many of you will have noticed the leader of the opposition was the last person to stop speaking. Different venue, same story." A titter broke out around the room and all eyes fell on Phyllis Stoppard. She shook her head and grinned generously. There were times to engage in hurling wisecracks and there were times to accept them graciously. She knew a jokey comment to begin with was often a good start to a speech or opening statement. It was water off a duck's back. Most of all, she was appreciative of being invited.

"Thank you to everyone for making the space in your diaries to attend at such short notice, but as the meeting unravels I'm sure you will see why that was necessary. The fact that I have felt the need to invite Phyllis along today shows the unusual and very important nature of what we are about to discuss. I have known Phyllis for a long time and contrary to what you might think from our sparring sessions across the Despatch Box and complete disagreement on our political views, I have an utmost respect for her as both a person and as a politician. That said, apart from her valuable input to this meeting, Phyllis is here because what we are about to discuss is bigger than party politics."

He briefly paused; a demarcation line as he got more serious.

"I am the Prime Minister and an experienced politician. Joy is the Home Secretary and an equally experienced politician, and she brought this matter to my attention. The fact that we could not conceive any acceptable solution to the problem we face other than to seek consensus from you today, will give you some idea of the scale of the matter I will lay out in a few seconds. You are quite rightly wondering why you are here. The answer is stark, and I have no intention of even attempting to soften the message."

Emphasis was required for the next line. Volume up, slow the speed and enunciate to perfection.

"Lives are at risk; millions of lives. The policy of not negotiating with those who would hold us to ransom is being tested. Our accepted view that capital punishment cannot be tolerated in our country is being challenged. Whilst you soak up those initial comments, let me tell you our provocateur is not an obvious terrorist, does not come from a radical or violent political group and has made no monetary demands on us. They want what they see as justice and have gone to extreme lengths to put us in a position where we need to give them our ear. It goes without saying that everyone in this room is subject to the Official Secrets Act and as such you cannot repeat what I am about to reveal. However, my reason for making such an obvious point, in case you were wondering, is that I have to make you understand you cannot, CANNOT under any circumstances, use this information once you leave here. One person has. They have paid a heavy price. They felt they acted in innocence, others might say it was naïve, but the outcome is the same. I will stand for my opening statement if you don't mind and I would prefer to be left to conclude before taking questions or views from the floor. As I proceed, I think many of your questions will be answered. We are joined via a video link by DCI Graeme King, who is in charge of this case, as I felt his knowledge might prove useful when you ask me those difficult questions later. I need a drink. Oh lovely; water!"

Astute presenter as he was, Peter Manger knew a few seconds for everyone to assimilate what he had laid out so far was a wise thing to do. The water was already poured, so he sipped a couple of times and then looked at the papers in front of him. The reverberation of a few whispers began as soon as he reached for his glass and then grew by degrees as others joined in. *What on earth could this be? Millions of lives and yet not a terrorist? Have you not heard any murmour's about this? PM and he doesn't know what to do? Has he lost it?*

When he felt the appropriate amount of time had been provided for those who needed to talk to get it out of their system, he looked up and the ripples of noise gradually calmed to total silence. He paused a few seconds to ensure he had total attention.

"Thank you. Following what appears to be a death by natural causes, a lady has approached the police to claim, what I can only describe as, some kind of responsibility. We have nothing definite yet, but there is evidence to suggest what she says could well be credible. The lady in question is one Eloise Langley, who many of you will know as the businesswoman or through her appearances on TV."

A muted gasp went up from several of the attendees. As very few of the people in that room had met her, the judgements they had made were based on what they saw on TV, read in the papers or perhaps heard when she was on radio. They would feel she was a well-spoken, educated and altogether nice lady. Now they were being told she might be a murderer!

"Yes, it's a shock to all of us when we first hear it. Many of you will know that Mrs Langley, through her business, provides the so called Chipsules that have caused something of a mini revolution in healthcare, and I will be surprised if no-one in this room has themselves, or doesn't know of someone who, has a Chipsule. Brace yourselves. Mrs Langley claims she can 'poison' any of these implants at will."

Another gasp, more animated this time, which quickly evolved into clusters of conversations breaking out. The excited hand gestures, the concern instantly expressed on faces and the words he heard being used were exactly as he expected. He raised his voice to keep the spotlight on him. There was more to come.

"The human emotion in you is to have your implants removed and to tip off those you know to do the same. That was exactly my reaction. We are not robots. Being in a position of influence and authority does not change the fact that, despite what the press might say, we experience the same emotions as the next man or woman. However, I must implore you not to do anything of that nature for two reasons. Mrs Langley has provided sound evidence that she can track each Chipsule and if they are removed in any significant numbers and she senses there has been a leak, she claims to have the capability to take matters into her own hands. I hope I do not need to spell out what that means, but just in case let me reiterate there are 5 million Chipsules currently active and that number is growing. The second reason, is that if we were to alert those around us to the potential danger, whilst our constituents, those in our chain of command and, in simple terms, millions of innocent people were left in peril, we would be abusing our positions. Choose whichever reason suits you best, but the only way forward is as a collective nation. Act in autonomy and from what I understand you might as well put a gun to the head of one or more people and pull the trigger. My conscience could not cope with that and if yours can, I suggest you should not be a part of this group."

Peter reached for his drink in part to wet his mouth and in part to let that sink in. He placed the glass down, ran his eyes round the table making glancing contact with as many people as possible and then continued.

"So to the demands being placed on us. Without going into too much detail, Mrs Langley had a son who was killed by a drunk driver several years ago. Many of you will recall the case I'm sure. She does not feel justice was served when the culprit, in her opinion, received only a minimal custodial sentence. Once again, her view is that the police could have handled the case better and that if the father of the convicted young man was not rich and well connected, the sentence would have been longer. To say that has irked her is something of an understatement. What she wants is for this man to stand trial again, however this time, and for this case only, capital punishment is to be available to the judge."

The room erupted in a cacophony of noise. It was to be expected. The subject of capital punishment is divisive at the best of times. Whilst many of those speaking out were clearly affronted by even the notion this was to be considered, a sizeable minority were less dismissive. On the contrary, they were voicing how this moment was always going to happen and instantly remembered their well-trodden phrases about why there was a place for it. Those in favour of the death penalty may hide in the backwaters, but given a modicum of interest and they gradually, cautiously, venture into the open, testing the current for likeminded souls.

Peter Manger tapped his pen on his water glass and the steady, repetitive chinking continued until everyone accepted they either shut up or that annoying sound will carry on.

"It would be disappointing if that happened again. This is not Prime Ministers Questions, we are not on the floor of the House and I have not invited a rabble. Please, conduct yourselves appropriately from now on."

His eyes were steely, his frown pronounced and his control of the congregation absolute once again.

"This is not a time to consider the pros and cons of capital punishment. That is considered periodically and has been rejected for very many years. As representatives of the people we accept that. Full stop. To get back to the matter at hand, the question is, do we hold true to our principles and say we will not negotiate with those who threaten us? Do we say the law is that capital punishment is not an option no matter what the circumstances? Several of us will have had to wrestle our consciences over that many times. Serial killers, child murderers, terrorists and the like. Strong arguments could be made for many of them to be put to death for the heinous crimes they committed. Like it or not, the difference this time is that the fate of millions lies in our hands. Your colleagues, your constituents, your friends and almost certainly, members of your family."

He looked down and took in a very large breath as he steadied himself for his final verbal salvo. The momentary pause built the tension.

"I absolutely know the right thing to do. I just do not know for definite what to do. Politicians must abide by their principles, leaders must show they are honest and true and all of us in this room have a responsibility to uphold the law. All of that rings loud in my ears. On the other hand, do we allow all of that to block out some obvious points. The choice, the apparent choice I must say, is the life of one, balanced against the lives of millions. The life in question is that of a convicted drunk driver who took the life of another. I have to look people in the eye and know I am worthy of being their Prime Minister. You, like me, will have to look people in the eye and explain with a clear conscience why you chose the decision you did. I would like you to take a moment to gather your thoughts. If it helps, imagine you have an irate parent in front of you asking why you chose someone lacking in moral qualities, a flawed individual, over the life of their child. Thank you."

Peter Manger sat down and without being too obvious, he surveyed the room to see if those in attendance were 'leaking' any clear views. A few were, as they sat upright with arms folded and were looking at others as if to say *What on earth is there to think about?* Others were leaning on their elbows and using their hands to conceal their eyes from an inquisitor. They, he assumed, were wrestling with their decision based on what he had laid before them. There were people with their eyes closed, possibly to vision the altercation he had painted for them. Others were staring, at the ceiling, the table or simply into space. Had they decided and were thinking this was all a waste of time or were they seeking some form of enlightenment from the focus of their gaze. He leaned forward.

"Right, questions or views please."

Phyllis Stoppard was first to speak.

"Thank you Peter. How concrete is your evidence that she can do what she says she can? I speak as both the leader of the opposition and a member of this invited group and if you want my support for anything other than what you called the 'right thing', I would need to make sure it was anything but flimsy."

"A very valid point Phyllis and you will not be the only person here thinking it. First of all, I should say that if we delay making a decision or if we intrude in any kind of identifiable manner, we might be goading her to act. She has said so in as many words. I have little concrete evidence, but before any of you judge me on that, please hear why I, and Joy, as I believe we speak as one voice on this, feel she is a credible threat." Joy Hamilton nodded vigorously.

"Mrs Langley reported a death and the police enquiries revealed there was enough reason to suggest the death may have been suspicious. A cabinet member used his knowledge to instigate the removal of Chipsules from his family members; Mrs Langley knew instantly and told DCI King at her local police station. She then provided the details of a member of the public who had the Chipsule removed, this time however, not through being tipped off by anyone party to what Mrs Langley was threatening. Anyone who has been involved with what we are discussing cannot have come to any other conclusion than Mrs Langley can track every Chipsule. As it stands we cannot by pass that, because we don't actually know how she is doing it. We are looking into that, but time is not on our side. To even attempt to intervene in however it is she tracks the Chipsules could tip her off to what we're doing. That said, her capability to turn every Chipsule into an agent of murder is another thing. She is intelligent, she has demonstrated some element of credibility and Joy tells me she has been one step ahead of us so far. I guess the question back to everyone here is, how much do you want proof of her credibility knowing that could cost lives?"

"If we were to concede that her demands be met, do we have a process to do that? Otherwise this is all bunkum and a waste of time." James 'Joc' Johnson, The Head of the Army, asked a typically pragmatic question.

Joy Hamilton spoke up. "I have looked into this briefly assuming it would come up today. There is no precedent in terms of creating a one-off law that goes against the accepted law of the land. However, we can fast track bills as you will all be aware. So, I am of the opinion that with enough support behind it, we can find a route to allow us to meet her demands if that is what we decide." Peter was pleased with Joy's response. Not only was it delivered with authority and confidence, but it also meant the meeting no longer had the feel of it being him, taking on everyone else. He had an ally.

DCI King then spoke. "Sir, am I permitted to ask a question?" Peter Manger looked at the screen on the wall of the head and shoulders of the local copper and said, "Of course, fire away."

"As with so many matters we come across I assume we can all agree the only way we know of the right or wrong answer is afterwards. So, as we have no crystal ball, can I ask for you to say what you want to happen? I just think that might speed things along a bit."

"Does anyone in the room have any burning questions to ask before I say my view? I will also ask Joy and DCI King for their views. No? OK then. Actually, let's start with you DCI King? What is your preferred route?"

Graeme King looked shocked as he was not expecting to speak first. The tables had been turned extremely rapidly. "Wow, not difficult to see why you're the Prime Minister!" A few chuckles from around the table, some genuine, some more supportive in nature, perhaps even sympathetic.

"I have spent quite a bit of time in the presence of Mrs Langley and got to know her fairly well. She is all the things the Prime Minister has said about her and more, and without any doubt I can say she is likeable. Yes, before you create a demon in your minds, let me state unequivocally that I like her. I think most people would, to be fair. However, she has been wounded. I cannot imagine what she went through losing her son and on top of that she feels his murderer, that is how she thinks of him, was too leniently dealt with and her view is that was because of the influence his father bought to bear. That would make any mother angry. The question then is, how far is the leap from angry to dangerous? As I have nothing to suggest the contrary, I presume we proceed on the basis that she has the mechanism to follow through on her threats. So, does she have the will? I would always tread carefully around a wounded animal and you can multiply that by any factor you like when it's a mother and she's protecting her children. Her son might be dead, but this is still her version of protecting him. On that basis I am inclined to believe she is capable of proving her intent if pushed. Would she murder millions of people, probably not? Does she have the metal, the inner mental strength to see off a few selected individuals to make you stand up and listen? I say again, I believe she does. From there, who knows?"

"Thank you Graeme. Joy?"

Joy Hamilton had nodded in agreement at much of what DCI king had said. Now it was her turn to voice an opinion.

"*Heaven has no rage like love to hatred turned, nor hell a fury like a woman scorned.* I appreciate it's widely considered this refers to a woman who has had her love rejected, but the sentiment can be used more widely and it fits in this instance. If we lost a child, then felt injustice, which turns to disdain for a system and at our fingertips we had the power, the capability to make people take note, wouldn't we? Having had some brief dealings with Mrs Langley, it's clear this was not done on a whim. It was well thought out, planned to a significant level of detail and took into perspective the actions of us as human beings. She knew that at some point we were likely to call her out on whether she could go ahead with her extortions. If she did not plan to show she could, why start this whole episode off? I say we proceed very cautiously. My view, a considered view, of which I have had the advantage over most of you in this room of several hours head start in thinking time, is to accede to her requests."

As soon as she had finished her sentence there were raised voices clearly unbelieving of what they had just heard. Whispers followed, loud enough to be a combined hissing, but individually quiet enough to not be identifiable to those purring them out. They were either questioning whether she was fit to be Home Secretary or quietly stating that her view was one that should be listened to carefully, before any dismissal of her conclusion.

Joy Hamilton coughed. A room made up of many who do not support your views is nothing new to a hardened politician, so she was not going to feel intimidation or give any sign she accepted disapproval. The clearing of her throat had also cleared the mutterings.

"We are here, because we have to make a decision. Before you make your stance, think carefully. I have changed my mind more than once on this, so my advice is to take a bit of time. Once you nail your colours to the mast you could get entrenched. Judge me all you like; others, and history, will judge you far more harshly depending on how this plays out."

She leaned back and aside from the creaking of her chair a dropped pin would have been heard. Peter Manger stroked his chin, his eyes staring at nothing as he chose his words.

"Thank you DCI King and you Joy."

He had time to prepare and rehearse his earlier words, but these would be off the cuff. There were signs of an inner battle going on inside his head about whether it was appropriate to deliver what was churning over in his head. One side of his mouth was raised up, smartly joined by the other side, he screwed up his nose. Then, the battle was over as he made a decision to talk from the heart.

"When my father died, I just wanted the world to stop. But it didn't. The postman carried his postbag up and down our street, the neighbours walked their dog, and everyone went on about their business exactly as they would on any day. BUT, this was not an ordinary day to me. My father had died. Perhaps some of you have experienced similar emotions when you lost a loved one. My loss was down to natural causes and old age. Over time I was able to move on and whilst I think about him every day still, I have accepted that dying is a part of living. Mrs Langley has not had the chance to move on, such has been the turmoil she has felt since the court case outcome. The obvious truth is, it's a good thing we cannot force others to listen when we suffer a loss. It is good we cannot affect other people's lives unduly, somehow try to put them on hold. It's good, because if we could, IF we had the power, IF we had the means, we might just do it. What we are discussing here is how to react to the intimidations of someone who can make others listen, who can affect others lives and who has been powerfully motivated by what they consider a tragedy of our justice process. Mrs Langley appears rational, but we do not know the level of mental disturbance she has felt, and is feeling. As I have already said, I know what I should do, but I am not sure what to do."

He took in a long, deep breath and then delivered his view.

"If we force her to show her hand, there is a chance we find out this was just an elaborate hoax. On mostly gut feel, it has to be reiterated, the unanimous feeling amongst those involved so far, is that is unlikely. Meaning she will kill an innocent person or any number of people. Or, we allow a judge to deliver a verdict on the guilt of one man for murder through dangerous driving. If guilty, we then accept we may have condemned him to die. That is what we do; the judge will make the verdict, but we will take responsibility for that death. On balance, and it has to be said with much wrestling of my thoughts, my view is we allow the re-trial and yes, we authorise the use of the death penalty. The means of which we will not even begin to discuss until there is a need. To ease my conscience if that were the case, and perhaps through my personal cowardice, I would approve every stay of execution I could as PM. It could take years, or perhaps forever, to get to the actual taking of life and that has helped in my decision making. I have seldom felt less confident that I am doing or saying the right thing, so to repeat what Joy said; judge me as you see fit. Then, come to peace with your decision."

He interlocked his fingers in front of him, his shoulders seemed to relax and deflate like a punctured beach ball and he seemed calmer now that he had opened up on his feelings about what to do. His intuition had always been good and he sensed people needed some time to reflect on what they had heard, be that through quiet consideration or through discussion with those whose views they trusted.

"If there are any more questions let's hear them now, before I propose a way forward."

Silence, shakes of the head and some heads down already getting their thoughts together.

"This has to be a personal decision, so confer, debate and converse with whoever you choose, as long as they are in this room right now. Once you have all the input, information and, within reason, the time necessary, make sure it is your choice you put forward. Abstaining cannot be an option. You need to be brave."

Peter Manger, with the steel of a seasoned statesman, swept the room for any sign of dissent to this. It might be uncomfortable to decide, but shirking was not for the body of people sat in these chairs around the table. If there was dissent, it was well hidden.

"By 1pm, can you all have emailed Robert Moore your view. If you choose to support your view with reasons, as I know some of you will like to do, that's fine. Assuming I have a clear majority, that is how I shall proceed. If not...............actually, I will not say as it might influence your decision. Thank you all for your attendance."

He rested his chin on his interlocked fingers as the congregation began to exit the room. He accepted the nods, the handshakes and the pats on his back in good spirit, knowing full well the position he had placed their deliverers in. He was pragmatic enough to know that meant those amiable gestures were accompanied by some cursing, just below the surface. When just Joy Hamilton was left, he thanked DCI King for his contribution and said either he, or Joy, would be in touch later that afternoon. Until then keep Mrs Langley comfortable, but do not let her know of what was discussed in the briefing room. She was clever and if she knew what was happening she might find ways to use it to further her demands. The screen went black as the DCI ended the call.

Peter Manger was not openly asking for any feedback on how he had handled the meeting, but like most people would want, Joy could tell he was keen to know how he had performed. She rose to her feet, strode over to the door and made sure it was firmly shut.

"And that, is why you are PM. Very well done, Peter. I was a little unsure when DCI King put us on the spot, but you handled that brilliantly and to be fair, he was right as it did save a lot of time."

The Prime Minister opened his eyes very wide, cocked his chin to one side and tilted his head to express how off guard he had felt when asked so directly for his view. Then he grinned or was it a grimace? She was unsure.

"Thanks Joy. I hope we get a clear vote as to what to do, but I presume you know what I will do if it is close?"

"You will follow the law of the land and the policy of her majesty's government." Sharp as a razor as ever, Peter was impressed with how quickly she summed situations up. There were three possible outcomes; a clear vote to yield to the demands, a clear vote to stick with current policy or, and least welcome, a close vote. That meant there was a 66% chance of it going against Mrs Langley.

"Joy, perhaps I shouldn't say this, but I just hope we don't procrastinate to a point where we annoy her, or she gets the notion we're stalling on purpose. If there is to be a loss of life, I sincerely hope it is not due to our inaction."

CHAPTER 20.

High jinks;
Playful activity.
'Hey-jinks' was a dice game in which one person would throw dice and have
to complete a task—such as drinking all the liquor in a cup. It shows up in
other writing from the late 1600s as both hey-jinks and high jinks.

Graeme King looked up from his computer screen, stood, and opened his blinds. He saw Mrs Langley arrive. As she was being led to the briefing room, she glanced in the direction of his office and gave him a wave. The sort of brief wave that was more to do with opening and closing the fingers than any noticeable movement of the hand. It was partnered with a slight movement of the lips and creasing around the eyes that created a grin of sorts. It was a greeting of familiarity, and while muted, it could have been taken for a greeting of intimacy. It was not lost on Rebecca Blades.
He reciprocated her wave almost as a reflex action and then looked away straight into the glare of DI Blades. Was she smirking? He beckoned her to join him with a jolt of his head and then moved away from the window. She strolled in and he pointed at the door, to indicate she should shut it.
"I like you Rebecca and believe it or not I wish I could openly discuss Mrs Langley's case with you. It helps my thinking to discuss cases with people I trust and respect and of course spreads the work. But, I cannot. Play this however you like, but understand my reasons are not anything to do with your competence or abilities as a copper. However, if you continue to sulk or give me evil stares, or do anything that might distract me from my job, then you should know the chances of you being involved in my inner circle going forward are extremely limited. That, would be a shame. Do you understand me?"
Her eyes were burning into him and she did not blink once, such was the intensity of her stare. Her head shook slightly as she broke her gaze and then proceeded to nod. Just once.

"Good. The damage your childish behaviour has done to our working relationship can be repaired over time, even though I am hacked off at your lack of trust in me. Stop your stupid conduct before you create any lasting damage. Now get out and do some work."

Rebecca Blades got up and left far more timidly than she had entered. She swung his door open, without letting it bang, and carefully paced her way back to her desk. She sat down, the heels of her hands holding up her head as she leaned forward onto her elbows. Shit! Her seated position was momentary, and then she was up again, heading for his office. She knocked and entered. DCI King had some designer reading glasses, matt black frames with red arms, which he used when he got fed up squinting. Stupid vanity. He took the arms off his ears and due to the design, he could then wrap the curved arms around the back of his neck and they stayed firmly in place. He acknowledged her presence, but without physically doing anything.

"Boss. Sorry." She looked childlike. Clearly, she loathed having to do this and was seeking his confirmation all was well between them now she had made the first move. He was the senior officer and it was incumbent on him to respond to her admission of being an idiot by letting her down gently. He held a firm, but non-threatening stare for a few seconds.

"There are many aspects of being a good police officer that you have yet to learn DI Blades, and right now one sticks out above all others."

She peered at him wondering what the hell she could have done now.

"Rebecca, you suck at apologies. You need some serious work at that. *Boss. Sorry.*" He mocked her voice. "Pathetic." Both held themselves in check briefly, but once one broke the other joined in the 'Ha' moment.

"One more thing DCI King.........you're a git." She turned on her heels, a renewed spring in her step and self-satisfied look on her face. She might not be intrinsically involved in the case, but she was back on good terms with the boss. He was her mentor, had been a terrific support in her career to date and he was one hell of an inspector to have on your side. However you slice it, she appreciated her working life was better under DCI King.

Graeme King took the glasses off and threw them on his desk. Time to brief Eloise, but without actually briefing her on anything that had happened earlier that morning or was happening right now. She was smart enough to know that several influential people were deciding her future, but he was not about to confirm it.

He greeted her as he entered with a 'Morning Eloise' and leant his rear end against a desk. She had looked up from her phone as he entered and acknowledged him with a pleasant smile.

"Go on Graeme, tell me someone has made a decision. No wait. I'll bet there is a committee being organised as we speak, but they need a meeting first to decide what kind of biscuits should be provided with the tea." His face rather gave away just how close to the truth she might be. His lapse was only fleeting, but she was onto it immediately. Her jokey air disappeared and she looked deep into his eyes, seeking to unearth the rest of the treasure she had stumbled across. Her eyes retracted into small slits as she tried to fathom out what was happening and what it was she had said that had caught him so off guard.

"Eloise, as you seem to have guessed, I have nothing new to tell you."

"Are we going to retain each other's trust or not DCI King?"

He knew exactly what she meant. Christ, she was so sharp. It was obvious she realised there was progress from last night and now she was using the bond they had built up to know exactly what that development was.

"Mrs Langley, as we're going all formal, based on our brief time of knowing each other, surprisingly or not, I like you. I can empathise with your situation and I hope our 'trust' can continue going forward. Assuming this all works out OK on your behalf, you will return to your business empire and live your privileged life. I, on the other hand, will still be a police officer and for the sake of my career, my pension and, in the short term, my salary, above all else I have to ensure my superiors trust me. There will be certain confidences I cannot break and of course things I will not be permitted to share with you. As and when that happens please do not ask me to choose between you and all the things I've listed. As I said, I like you, but I love my job, most of the time, and I love my family and all this career provides for them. You are clever enough to know our relationship has its limitations. You said you hoped I would be involved in your case, which I took as a compliment at the time, but if you hoped it was because I was likely to be weak and easily rolled over, then you will be disappointed."

Her face eased out of concentration into a gentler demeanour. Playful even.

"DCI *Graeme* King," she emphasised his first name as a retort to his 'formal' quote, "You say you like me, then you say, 'our relationship' and you end with 'easily rolled over'. What's a girl to think, are you chatting me up, because those lines are very rough around the edges?"

His discomfort at her insinuation manifested itself in a reaction that catapulted him away from the desk as he also launched into a denial, but she was enjoying teasing him.

"Absolutely not, and......"

"*Absolutely not,* well let me down gently why don't you. What's so wrong with me that you would phrase it like that?"

"Nothing. There is nothing wrong with you."

"Is that another chat up line, because it's not too strong on charm."

"Let me start again...."

"You want to start a new set of chat up lines?"

"No! I want to clarify what I said. What I meant was........."

"I know perfectly well what you meant Graeme. Sorry, being in this bloody room for this many days is sending me stir crazy."

He leaned back on the desk relieved. In this day of political correctness, at which he was far from adept at, he knew how much trouble he could be in for saying the wrong thing to the wrong person. He dropped his head onto his chest and looked down at the floor as he crossed one leg over the other. His mind was letting his body relax again. He had taken the bait hook, line and sinker. He smirked to himself and then turned his head to the side facing Eloise.

"There I was, thinking you're a nice person, a good person and all the while, just below the surface, is pure evil."

The twinkle in his eye told her he could see the funny side of her prank.

"Graeme, I do trust you and I apologise for attempting to take liberties. I will try not to do that again, but if I do, please shut me down quickly. Am I forgiven or is it the handcuffs and shackled in a cell for the rest of my stay?"

"If you think I am going to answer any sentence with the phrases, 'handcuffs' and 'shackled' in it, after your last little stunt, you are sadly mistaken."

He got up and headed for the door.

"As soon as I know anything, I'll let you know. I would like to have a way forward, nearly as much as you. If for no other reason than I can get my briefing room back."

CHAPTER 21.

Bite the bullet.
Accept the inevitable impending hardship and endure the resulting pain with
fortitude.
Patients undergoing surgery would be given a stick of wood or a pad of leather
to bite on in order to concentrate their attention away from the pain and also
to protect against biting their own tongues. A bullet, being somewhat
malleable and not likely to break the patient's teeth, is said to have been an
impromptu battlefield alternative.

At 1.05pm, Robert Moore entered the PM's office. He had the results of the vote from the meeting earlier that morning. All bar 3 people had voted to proceed with Mrs Langley's request for a new trial and, with it, a one-off possible sentence of death available to the judge. He placed the document on the PM's desk and on a separate page were the reasons given by those who chose to validate their decision. The more streetwise members of the group, or perhaps those who had been burned before, chose not to give reasons, probably knowing this could come back and be hung around their neck like an Albatross depending on how things panned out. Who knows why others had chosen to air their views; to suck up to the PM, to ease their conscience, or perhaps it was their habit to do just that.

Peter Manger did not even look at the comments. There was a clear majority and that was all he was concerned about. He breathed in deeply, contemplating the magnitude of the decision that had been agreed. Up to this point in his premiership there had been no stimulus to give an order to go to war or involve the armed forces in any major military conflict, but he assumed it would feel very similar to this, if not exactly the same. A life, or lives, were at risk due to a commitment he would make. It was a heavy responsibility, but no-one took the top job in politics unaware of their obligation in making such decisions.

Having the time to reflect and ponder, is often not a luxury prime ministers have, so he immediately began planning with Robert Moore the steps to be taken and the clear obstacles that lie ahead;

A conference call to all ministers, informing of the decision that had been taken and asking for their support. Cabinet members to be invited, their attendance was not optional.

An announcement to the House of Commons.

The leader of the House of Lords to do the same.

Calls to the owners and editors of all newspapers and major news channels. He would request a tempering of any instinct to sensationalise this story.

How can parliamentary sovereignty be used to challenge the EU laws they would be contradicting? The threat of continued membership was no longer an issue and the British public could not wait for the bureaucrats to make a decision.

The list was long.

Once all the minsters had been briefed and he had spoken to media editors, someone had to tell Jonas Rafferty what was happening. This young man was totally oblivious to any of what was materialising and had no idea his liberty, or indeed his life, were now in peril. There would be a challenge as to how lawful this was; human rights were clearly an issue. Who knows what else Mr Rafferty senior would bankroll his legal team to unearth to stop this going ahead. Peter Manger would have paid any amount to protect his own children, so he completely understood what would happen and why. Joy Hamilton would be asked to brief the Rafferty's lawyer, who in turn would speak to Jonas and his family.

Joy would also speak to Superintendent Jeremy Day and his Chief Constable, Gordon Mackay. Both were to stay in the background and support DCI King as the case developed. Ahead of that she would inform Graeme King of the decision, so that Mrs Langley would know soonest. This was going public and that meant she would never go back to her previous life. She was already used to being in the spotlight, but this was on another level. Every aspect of her life would be scrutinised and her privacy, as it was, would be a thing of the past. Careful what you wish for, Peter Manger thought to himself. The prize she sought was huge for her and her family. He just hoped she had realised the price she would pay for seeking it.

CHAPTER 22.

Chance your arm;
To take a risk.
In the military, rank is worn on the arm. To chance your arm meant to put
your rank at risk by undertaking an action which could lead to promotion (if
successful) but demotion (if a failure).

Following his call from the Home Secretary, Graeme King made his way to inform
Eloise Langley of the outcome. However, before he did so he had enquired of Joy
Hamilton as to what his role was now. Was he to proceed treating Mrs Langley as a
suspect for a murder? If so, had the situation around her arrest and detention
changed at all? If he was not to proceed, what about the possible murder of Harry
Vaughan and her threat to so many other people, unspecified other than they had a
Chipsule implanted?
As it stood there was little evidence to charge her with regarding Harry's demise,
other than her own sketchy admission. But even that was shrouded in doubt, as her
statement was all smoke and mirrors, nothing definite. As for the threats, a
conviction would need to show it was credible, real and imminent. Mrs Langley was
one smart operator and she probably knew where she would cross the line and right
now, it was very likely she had not done so.
Joy threw it back at DCI King for a recommendation. He gave her his view. He still
had the passport, so she was going nowhere. The local police to Harry Vaughen,
should make further, gentle, enquiries about his behaviours and physical symptoms
leading up to his death. If there was real suspicion and indications of obvious foul
play, a post-mortem could be authorised. This was only going to happen with Home
Office approval, as the Vaughen family were still grieving and the current extent of
gentle interest in how he died was going to be upsetting enough, without digging
him up to examine his body.

Depending on how Mrs Langley reacted to the news he was to give her, DCI King would make a further recommendation to the Home Secretary based on how he perceived the level of risk for those with Chipsules fitted. His gut instinct was it would be low to negligible. If it was not, neither appeared to have a solution for what to do. Eloise held all the cards. Stick or twist? Force her to show her hand and they risked getting the proof she had claimed she could provide; the dead body of an unsuspecting individual. She really was causing some head scratching. With only scant reason, founded on the flimsiest of evidence, if it could even be called that, she was causing huge legal decisions to be made. The media would go into a feeding frenzy when they found out she had not been charged with a crime up to this point.

* * *

Eloise took on board all that Graeme King was telling her. She would get her trial. The death of Harry Vaughen would be investigated further, and it was likely a decision about her threats to multitudinous people would be taken further after the trial. He examined her face and body language for signs of pleasure or perhaps relief. She had won, after all. But, she just took it all in. Her eyes produced several verses of flitting up, down, left and right, but for each chorus they returned to focus on him. She was taking this all in, as if ticking off some checklist in her head to make sure nothing had been missed. After about a minute she spoke.
"When?"
"When what?"
"When will the trial be?"
"I don't know. There are a lot of procedures to go through and many of them are heading through unchartered waters, so.......... months I guess." He was unprepared for the question. In his mind she would be super pleased with her victory and realise the machinery of the court system would take time to put in motion. His answer was accompanied by an exaggerated shoulder shrug, hands raised as if carrying something imaginary in his hands and a withdrawing of the lips. These unnecessary, but apparently uncontrollable, dramatics displayed his discomfort at being caught off guard.
"That's unacceptable."
"*Unacceptable!* Eloise, you have what you wanted. The trial is going ahead, are you sure you shouldn't just let things take their course now?"
"I did that before at the first trial and got shafted. Remember? If I ever got this far, I assumed there would be stalling tactics and the Rafferty family will do all they can to disrupt procedures; they do have a track record. So no, I want the time scale to be of

an absolute minimum."

"If you were the PM or Mr Rafferty, junior or senior, you would want to stall too." It was an emotional outburst, delivered without the use of a filter. Without a flicker to indicate his comment had riled her, Eloise responded.

"Let me deal with the people you have mentioned. If I were PM, I would not rest until the law of this land was fair for all and not biased in favour of the rich and powerful. As for Mr Rafferty junior, a drunk, a reckless driver, he will get no pity from me and deserves all that is coming his way. Mr Rafferty senior defended his son as if he had done nothing wrong, then spent his money and used his influence to get Jonas off lightly. Given the time, he will do exactly the same thing again. Well, let us see him do that in a far more restricted time frame."

"If you push too far, you might lose the re-trial. Why not wait?"
Her serenity was waning.

"Graeme, listen carefully. That trial takes place within a time that I find acceptable or you and the people you represent will be inviting me to prove I can follow through on my threats. I risked everything when I walked in here originally, so no warnings or ultimatums are going to influence or scare me. The promise of a trial, is not a trial. The possibility of a judge sentencing that murderer to death, is not the same as a noose squeezing the life out of him. No games Graeme. Tell whoever you need to, but the trial takes place at my speed, not theirs."

There may have been a discernible tremble in her voice, but the passion it was conveyed with, and the white-hot hate emanating from every pore as she spoke, left him in no doubt about her determination to get what she wanted.

"OK. When would you like the trial to take place?"
"Within one week."

Graeme King felt an uncontrollable jerk in his head as he heard what she said. On what planet was this woman living? The organisation required to set up a court trial such as this was no quick process. The legal issues to be wrangled over would take months in any normal situation and that was before the civil rights brigade got to hear of how the law, as we know it, was being rode roughshod over. Was she being serious?

He searched for a clue to help answer his own question. Never had he seen someone speak with their whole body in the way she was now. The eyes steady as a rock, not a flinch, pure intensity. Veins were prominent in her neck and forehead and from the neck down the lack of any perceivable movement, spoke volumes. She was serious alright.

Then it occurred to him. Who would have given her a cat in hell's chance of getting this far and yet, heaven and earth were being moved to accommodate her, or at least seeking to pacify. Based on that, why wouldn't she keep pushing? What was sure, was that she would have foreseen the timescale for the trial being an issue if she got to this juncture.

"Before I leave this room and pass on your request, can I just check that you have thought through the ramifications of what you're asking? Eloise, any goodwill you have generated will be lost and you could be making the chances of achieving your ultimate goal so much more difficult. I would urge you to reconsider."

"Goodwill? Nice try Graeme, but seriously, I don't think I have much of that to use up. I have been thinking about little else beyond the ramifications of what I'm doing since I started out on this, and that was several months ago. I cannot have my family left in limbo for months, probably years based on what I have experienced, wondering what will happen to me. A week they can cope with, much more and then I'm adding to their hurt. Plus, you and I know full well that the people making decisions about me and what I want would like nothing better than long periods of inaction. That is not how this is going to work."

She was right of course. From the setting up of a public enquiry, through to organising the date for a trial, the wheels of the legal system ground very slowly, but for good purpose. When personal liberty or reputation are at stake, slowly, slowly, trumps act in haste, repent at leisure every time. Also, whilst the individual passions of those immediately involved might never dwindle, the wider public ire at injustices, or acts of monstrous cruelty causing terrible pain, would reduce from leaping flames, to red embers. The sparks could jump up again, but the original fire was unlikely to be renewed once enough time had passed. Any delays meant those judgements perceived as unpalatable to those who felt wronged, might generate some ill feeling, but rioting on the street was not going to happen.

DCI King was nothing if not persistent.

"What about collecting evidence, briefing witnesses, putting a jury together?"

"The evidence remains the same for the last trial. Some dusting off to do, but nothing new to mull over that I am aware of. Same for the witnesses and their statements. Request volunteers for the jury, I doubt you'll be short of takers. You can keep thinking of problems and I can keep overcoming them, or, you can call your bosses. To help them see clearly through the mists, can you remind them that the only way I can prove how serious I am is to kill somebody and I can be very choosey about who that is."

A resigned slouch of the shoulders and drooping of the chin onto his neck were the tell-tale signs that he was not comfortable with her decision. He was equally aware any further protests were futile. With nothing more to say, he opened the door, gently closed it behind him without turning around and stepped out towards his office.

Eloise was determined to give off the impression of being totally in control, resolute and strong. Yet she could feel her heart was pounding, going so fast. She wondered if her neck was displaying red blotches, an indication of stress that had been uncomfortably obvious in her younger days. This was all so alien to her. Talking about killing people, making demands that would be seen as incredulous upon first hearing and having to concentrate so hard on everything she did and said. There was to be no weakness shown, no chink of light that could give the impression she was not committed to her cause and capable of the unimaginable killing of the masses. She was used to focusing on complex information for long periods in her business world, but that was about money. The pressure was incomparable to when your own liberty and another person's life are at risk. She liked Graeme, but even so, she was very conscious of never dropping her guard and showing any mental frailty, any likelihood of compromise in her demands, when conversing with him. He was the eyes, ears, basically the antennae of those who would rule on her case. He was also likely to be a big influencer on whatever they did. As such he, and through him they, needed to know she was committed to her cause and also capable of being a danger to other human beings.

CHAPTER 23.

Bandy about;
Toss words around.
"Bandy" originated from an Old French word "Bander", which was used in an
early form of tennis and meant to "hit a ball to and fro". Later, in the early
17th century, "Bandy" became the name of an Irish team game from which
hockey evolved. The ball was "bandied" back and forth between players.

"She wants what?"

Joy Hamilton had accepted the call from DCI King. When he had begun by saying she was not going to like this, she excused herself from the meeting with some LGBT community leaders, who were concerned about the visit of a head of state who supported his countries ban on any homosexual behaviour. Her Minister for Equalities would step in for her whilst she took the call.

Once in the sanctuary of her office, she told him to hit her with the latest request from Mrs Langley.

"And you have told her that is impossible?"

"I have."

"And?"

"And... we will have blood on our hands if we don't. The thing is, she thinks we're playing for time and she is not prepared to stand for that."

He went on to relay her being 'picky' message, which was clearly meant as a threat to the decision makers in this whole cat and mouse game. Give me what I want or explain to your partner why their brother is now dead, or something along those lines. Graeme King passed on the message about how she could overcome any obstacles put in the way. If evidence of her ability to reach out and strike someone down was needed, she could readily comply.

Joy Hamilton took a moment. This woman was one step ahead all the while. Eloise Langley had clearly anticipated what the normal responses would be, the desired routes to follow and then she had set the challenge for those in positions of authority to find a way around them. The more she kept the timeframe short, the more she was in control, because they were not being given any leeway to check out how valid her claims were. Before Joy reported in to the PM she wanted to be sure she had done all she could. Time to put a little pressure on the other way and see what response that had.

"Graeme, please do not take this as any slight on your involvement so far, but if you don't mind I would like to speak direct to Mrs Langley again."

Whether he minded or not, when the Home Secretary makes a request like that, albeit more of a statement of what will happen than any sort of supplication, he could only grin and comply. He asked if another video link should be set up and Joy Hamilton said, "No, give her your phone now. Let's move this along."

Eloise Langley looked up as DCI King entered the briefing room that had become her home from home when visiting the station. He made her aware the Home Secretary would like to discuss her latest demand. Eloise combed his face for any clues as to what he knew about the agenda for this call. He was not looking at her. He handed the phone in her direction, having put it on speaker first, and gave absolutely nothing away. Perhaps that was all he knew.

"Hello Home Secretary, it's Eloise Langley here."

"Hello Mrs Langley. You've upped the ante just a little with your request for a trial within a week, but I'm sure you knew the reaction it would have. Before I speak to the PM, there are a couple of points I would like to make. IF, and that is a massive 'if' I should say, we can move heaven and earth to meet your deadline, I will be asking DCI King to formally investigate your involvement in the death of Harry Vaughen and to charge you with threatening behaviour on a grand scale. You will be detained immediately and not released until it is considered safe for the public at large for this to happen."

There was a silent void for several seconds. Then Eloise spoke.

"Were you asking for me to reply?"

"Please."

"Do you know who Faye Parker is? Let me help you. She is 18 years old, soon off to university having secured good A level results. She is a talented musician, pianist I believe, and has represented her county at Netball. She had a Chipsule implanted 1 year and 3 months ago following some dizziness she was encountering, which her GP felt might be down to some blood related issues. If you look closely enough you will see there are some similarities to my son Tobias, at the time of his death. Scrub that. MURDER. Age, Uni etc., However, there are also some clear differences. For example, he was not the niece of the serving Prime Minister."

The air seemed to vacate the room. A tingling on the arms of Graeme King was followed by the coldness of goose bumps. There was no sound at all on the phone. No breathing, no sighing, just the background sound of an air con unit humming away.

"You do like to play hardball, don't you."

"I do not like being given ultimatums intended, I presume, to persuade me to slow things down and play it more your preferred way. That will not happen. My life, and that of my remaining family, has been disrupted enough over the past few years and the sooner this is resolved the better. Now, before you follow through on your course of action, do you want to speak to the PM?"

She handed the phone back to DCI King and as he went to take it she gripped it tightly, causing him to look directly at her. The stare was deep and intense and she held his eyes in a frozen grip for a few seconds before letting go of the phone. However, the stare was not released for a while longer. He was slightly taken aback, but disengaged himself from her glare and left the room. As he did so he asked the Home Secretary to refrain from speaking until he was back in his office.

He fairly galloped across the floor and shut his door with a bit more force than he had intended. The semi slam indicated to Joy Hamilton that he had returned to his office.

"Are you alone Graeme?"

"Yes."

"In the world of David Attenborough, that would have been like an Antelope playing chicken with a Lion. I took a gamble and now I'm in a whirl about what to do again. If I tell you to detain her, not only does it sound petty, but also, I'm risking lives. Well certainly that of Faye Parker. But, with this going public soon, she can't be allowed to wander about free as a bird. Have you any indication of how she can possibly turn these Chipsules into grim reapers from within your station?"

"I have given that a lot of thought and all I can come up with is that she has help on the outside. There could be a list of names, ranked for maximum effect, and if she does not return home every night, or some other agreed indicator that everything is proceeding to plan, the other party can activate the Chipsule to become a lethal weapon."

"Any idea who that, or perhaps even who they, could be?"

"I could soon produce names of the more obvious candidates, but there comes with that a couple of reasons that have precluded me from doing so to this point. Firstly, the list of people who feel justice has failed them is very long and many of those people would not give up the chance to give the system a real hard slap across the face. Secondly, and forgive me for saying this so soon after your altercation with Mrs Langley, but if she finds out we're digging, then I could be the one that tips her over the edge to show what she is capable of. As the saying goes, the trouble with grabbing a Tiger by the tail is that sooner or later you have to let go. Every so often she hints at what that could mean and we have no way of knowing if she can, or cannot, use these Chipsules as a murder weapon."

"OK Graeme, I'm open to suggestions. Do you have any?"

"Yes Ma'am, I mean Joy."

"You can call me Fluffy if you like, I just hope you've got something good."

"I would explain what will happen when the media gets wind of this and the impact on her son, Andrew, who seems to be why she wants things to proceed as normally as possible for him. Not upsetting his 6th form work etc. Then give her one more day as a 'visitor', to allow her to make whatever arrangements she needs to for him and then we detain her the next day. We both know she will thank us in the long run, because TV crews and journalists camped outside the gates is no fun for anybody."

"Go chat to her and come straight back to me. Well done Graeme. What a turn up. The female Home secretary goes in tough and gets a bloodied lip and the burly copper suggests a more sensitive way. Let's hope your way works. Go."

Graeme began his suggested way forward to Eloise, by explaining it was, in his view, the right thing to do for her family. As a well-known face, Eloise might have some insight into how the mercenary hacks and paparazzi operate, but for a story like this she would not be able to grasp how the media would invade every tiny detail of her private life. What they could not find out, they would make up themselves. Like it or not, the truth was a poor second when it came to getting viewers or selling stories. Then he laid out his plan. Eloise had one day to find somewhere for Andrew to live. It needed to be out of the reporters clutches and with someone who could reassure him, if necessary, that what was being reported was not to be believed. Then she would remain in custody, whilst enquiries continued. He openly stated the police's reputation, and his, were definitely a factor in what he suggested. They were in danger of becoming a laughing stock as and when the news broke about a potential murderer being allowed home each day. However, he reiterated that it was in Andrew's best interests not to have to force himself through battalions of journalists, brandishing microphones and shouting horrible questions to get a reaction, every time he left or arrived home. If there was no compromise from her, it meant someone having to make a tough decision on his side. That could force her hand. If she wanted that, then dismiss his idea. If not, she had not lost any momentum and hopefully she did not have to consider taking any lives, for the time being at least.

In his line of work, Graeme King had become an expert on body language and how people reacted when they needed to do some serious thinking. Usually, it was when he had some toe rag by the short and curlies and he was offering them the chance to drop a few of the more major players in the smelly stuff in return for him putting a good word in with the judge. On those occasions the eyes darted everywhere, they became fidgety, foot tapping, knee bouncing, head rested on the table, then flung back and they covered their face with clammy hands. The pressure was too much for them and they struggled to make a decision. Eloise on the other hand was still. No outward signs of feeling any pressure at all. Her eyes were the only things that moved and even they were deliberate movements.

Eloise was practiced in making big decisions and she had a way of doing this from her business world. She could quickly way up the pros and cons of situations without giving any clues as to which way she would go. So many people had said what a good Poker player she would have been. Up to now, it usually meant financial considerations, so this was completely different. But the conclusion strategy had become a habit to her and not one that was easy to break even if she wanted to. She had calculated there was a good chance her freedom would be removed at some point, so his proposal was no great surprise. Andrew was keen to keep on seeing his friends for as long as possible, but had accepted a plan B was required. He would now go and live with her close friend, Stephanie Hurst, and be home schooled by private tutors. He knew it was going to happen, just not when, and he also knew it was very likely to be at short notice. The only thinking she was having to do was how to make this seem like it was a 'new' problem for her, and not one she had guessed would happen and had already dealt with it. She wanted to have some bargaining power.

"OK. It's not ideal, but I'll go along with your suggestion. Honesty, and a brain, now you see why I was hoping to get you on my case."

He looked marginally flustered by her comments of praise for him and in typical fashion, rather than acknowledge what she had said he carried straight on to avoid needing to respond.

"Excellent, so let's get down to the details of it……"

"On one condition."

Here it comes. Another bolt from the blue just he as he thought he was making headway.

"I want to attend the trial. Obviously I'd expect to be escorted by one or more of your officers, but no handcuffs. My family will be watching and I do not want them to be upset if I'm presented as some criminal."

"Aren't you though?"

"Am I? Until you can show me some proof to that effect, I would like to be treated as an innocent person helping my local police with their enquiries."

"I can't see why that should be an issue, so unless you hear differently from me that's fine. Eloise, go and make your arrangements and then tomorrow when you come back it will be interview rooms and a cell as opposed to this briefing room. OK?"

She licked her lips seductively.

"Can I request that you tuck me in each night?"

"How the hell can you still be messing about at a time like this?"

"Tuck me in tomorrow night and I'll tell you."

"Eloise...."

"Graeme, you passionate beast. Please wear a uniform."

"As I was saying, Eloise, get out of here and I'll see you in the morning. Before you go, can I ask why you feel the need to try and make me feel uncomfortable with these innuendo's?"

The comment took her by surprise and she went on the defensive.

"Like you've never made a woman feel 'uncomfortable' with a few suggestive comments."

"I'm surprised. You're telling me this is payback for things you think I may have said or done?"

She had made an irrational, impulsive throwaway remark and he had caught her out.

"My apologies Graeme, truth is it's probably nerves coming out and helping me deal with all this. It won't happen again. I wasn't thinking."

"Point is this. I'm not sure if our paths would have crossed had you not got yourself into all this, as we do mix in very different social circles. If we had, I think we would have gotten along well as friends. I have a rule of thumb about whether people are the sort I should consider as friends when I start to get to know them. It's very simple; would my wife like them? She's a far better judge of character than me you see."

"Subtle as a brick Graeme. Point made. I will not cross the line and who knows I may buy you and your wife a nice meal at some point. She's a lucky lady."

"Eloise, just look at me." His hands rose in a sweeping movement all the way up his body, stopping just below his neck. "The luck is all mine."

As she left the police station Eloise cursed herself. Damn it. Trying to be funny and you let your guard down. *Nerves coming out* indeed. No more slips. Get back on course woman. Chat to Stephanie and sort Andrew out for his stay at hers. Give the legal team a green light to establish a way the case could be heard under the murder banner. They had been given clear instructions; whether the likelihood of that was good or not, she wanted them to make an awful lot of noise about it. Then, enjoy a long bath and finally, a nice meal with her son. They would order in, his choice; Chinese or Indian.

CHAPTER 24.

Blood is thicker than water;
Family bonds are closer than those of outsiders.
The origin of the expression blood is thicker than water is hotly debated. Some
believe that the roots of this phrase go back to Germany in the 1100s, or even
to the Talmud. However, many believe that blood is thicker than water is a
proverb first collected in An Excellent Collection of the Best Scotch Proverbs,
compiled by Allan Ramsay in 1737.

The Prime Minister had been visibly shaken by the thinly veiled threat on his niece as Joy took him through all that had happened since his last update. His thoughts instantly went to protecting her, but how could he? If he tipped her off and the Chipsule was removed, Eloise Langley would know and she would simply put the finger on someone else. That would obviously be another member of his immediate or extended family. He was powerless and because of that, angry. The enormity of what he was facing as the serving Prime Minister had not been lost on him, quite obviously, but once it became personal it magnified several times. The vision was sharper with enhanced colours, the sound acute and the emotions heightened to the distraction of almost anything else, including reason. He sounded off at Joy Hamilton about how these Chipsules could be fitted, promoted and paid for by his government, without proper risk assessments being undertaken. She pointed out that all the appropriate risks had been assessed, but how could they know there was a chance of them being used to kill people?

Peter Manger began to calm down, just a little, as Joy took him through what was being agreed. He knew, and Joy knew, they were anything but in control of this situation. However, hot heads were not going to help, or change, the state of affairs. They discussed what had happened and what was happening next. All ministers were in the know. The Rafferty solicitor had been told and been given specific instructions to brief his client within 24 hours at the latest. An announcement was being made to the House of Commons tomorrow afternoon, with a live screening to the House of Lords. All media outlets would receive a copy of the speech thirty minutes ahead of him entering the chamber, but with an embargo on airing it until he had sat down. A recently retired judge had been approached and he had accepted the invitation to hear the case. The papers had been dispatched to him and he was getting up to speed as they spoke.

Peter Manger was still feeling angry at the involvement of his niece, who was totally innocent and just happened to be related to him. However, despite his own personal feelings, he was well aware this was a comparative calm before the storm. Soon there would be the Rafferty family protestations, followed by the media circus that would soon erupt and then he could expect attacks from all sides.

Imagine being Jonas Rafferty. He had served the time he was sentenced to, and whether you agreed with his penalty or not, fact was he had paid the piper and had assumed all this was behind him. Not only was it very much ahead of him, now he was facing the death penalty.

As a father he could empathise with Reginald Rafferty. It was said one of the cruellest fates to befall a parent is to lose a child; no-one should live to see their child die. Of course, Eloise had been through this and clearly it did not seem as if she would offer any sympathy to her persecutors as they were the direct cause of so much public and private pain for her. That said, Mr Rafferty senior was going to have to watch his son's grip on life being decided in front of him.

Then there were the newspaper columnists who would freely offer views to stoke the fire from the comfort of their laptops. Radio news presenters would ask for interviews with ministers and, as usual, overlook any good or positive reasons for decisions being made and focus on what could go wrong with what had been decided. TV news and political programmes would invite experts with differing views to hopefully create a heated discussion and of course generate great viewing numbers. Peter Manger chose his profession, so he had to accept how the game was played, but he would have his say on the preening, self-satisfied, parasites of the media in due course. They were paid two or three times his salary as PM, they had no responsibility for the impact their interviews/stories might have and yet they sat in judgement on politicians. His memoirs would pull no punches.

CHAPTER 25.

Over a barrel;
Helpless, in someone's power.
It alludes to the actual situation of being draped over a barrel, either to empty
the lungs of someone who has been close to drowning, or to give a flogging.
Either way, the position of helplessness and in being under someone else's
control is what is being referred to.

Reginald Rafferty was in total disbelief. His solicitor had just finished explaining what would be happening. Reg had not comprehended much of it as there was an information overload from the point he heard, *new trial with a potential for the death penalty.* Jonas broke down in tears as he began to appreciate what was being said, so his mum, Carla Rafferty, had her arms around his shoulders to comfort him. Both expected Reg, as the dad, to sort this all out, to make it go away. He could not think straight. His son sobbing, his wife looking at him with expectant eyes and the pressure he suddenly felt in that room was too much. He told Simon Burgess, his lawyer, to walk with him in the garden so he could clear his head.

"Simon, you did a stunning job for Jonas at the last trial, so what can we do this time?"

"Reg, right now I have no idea. I have only just found out myself, so formulating a strategy has not happened. My initial thought would always be to stall, so we can build the best case possible and of course seek ways to discredit the prosecution case. However, it was made loud and clear to me that I could try to delay proceedings, but our chances were limited due to the rate of knots everything to do with this is moving."

"Does that mean there is 'some' possibility then."

"The way 'limited' was presented to me, suggests it's more of a no possibility."

"Money is no option Simon, get this sorted. They can't just drag him into court at short notice for a charge he has already served time for."

"Normally, you would be right. However, this Mrs Langley has found a way to have a massive influence on how this is playing out. When I protested at the way this was being handled and I threw the laws of the land at them, I was told the laws are being re-written for this case alone. We will find out what her game is tomorrow apparently, when the PM delivers a statement to parliament. Until then I was told to merely brief Jonas, and you of course, and then prepare for court. In twenty-seven years, I thought I had pretty much seen anything and everything that could happen regarding the law, but this is as fresh and new as it gets."

Reg grabbed Simon by the arm and gently pulled him round so they were facing each other.

"Are you telling me, my son will be tried in a case where process is being made up as we go along and that on top of that the death penalty is being permitted for his case only?"

"Not quite that simple, but in effect, along those lines."

"Well, do something. Who can we appeal to? There must be someone or some council somewhere."

"I know this is difficult to take on board when it's so emotional for you, but as I've said, we have to wait for the PMs address to the House of Commons tomorrow and then hopefully we can decide our best route to prevent this trial going ahead."

This could not be happening to his family. Reg Rafferty was a man who got what he wanted, always had. He called in favours from people in authority, shelled out a bunch of cash or lent on those who needed leaning on. Yet here he was, with the most important situation he had ever had to face, and he had no idea what to do. The only advice he had was to wait for some speech, no way was he doing that. He headed back into his house and marched straight into his study having said good-bye to his lawyer. As they had shook hands at the door, Reg made it crystal clear he expected Simon to be in touch as soon as possible after the PM had spoken to parliament. There was a little more force in the hand squeeze than normal and a bit more steel in the look; message received and understood.

He had to do something. He called Gordon Mackay, the Chief Constable, who he had been on a number of charity fundraising events with. The call rang a few times, but then went to answerphone. He called the office number he had. A lady answered;

"Chief Constable Mackay's office."

"Hello, this is Reginald Rafferty. Can I speak to Gordon please?"

"One moment."

One moment turned into 2 minutes, then three and then, just as he was getting completely fed up of that horrid looped music, the lady who had answered his call came back on.

"So sorry to have kept you, Chief Constable Mackay is unavailable right now."

"Can he call me back please?"

"He is very busy, so I cannot guarantee it."

The tone was firm, formal and lacking in warmth. No frills, minimum information provided as expediently as possible.

"Wait a minute, is he unavailable to everyone or just me?"

No response.

"OK, I get it. Chief Constable or not, I am not a man to make enemies with and I do not take to this kind of behaviour very well. You pass that on."

"Thank you for your call."

The line went dead. A sense of loneliness came over him. People were being warned off from speaking to him. Why? What exactly was going on here? All those business deals he had been involved in, where people were only too willing to move mountains for him, did not matter a jot to what was at stake here. Yet, he was being frozen out.

He went back to the TV room, as they called it. Jonas had stopped crying, but he was still very distressed. His excess tears had drained into his nose mixing with his mucus and causing a steady stream. When hearing the revelation of what lied ahead, snot was the last thing on his mind. Now, as he calmed down just a little, he was more mindful of it, so he wandered off for a blow at the point his father returned.

Carla was sitting on her own and looked up as he came in. He knew she hoped he had something good to tell her, but his briefest eye contact and shaking of the head told her there was nothing she wanted to hear. He landed heavily in one of the armchairs.

"That bloody woman. Jonas has done his time, so what's the point in dragging it all up again? The thought of another trial must be upsetting for her. Why can't she just move on?"

Carla looked at her husband. She loved him very much, but at times he was a spoilt brat of a grown up.

"Would you?" Her enquiry was delivered with a soft voice, but had the belt of a heavyweight boxer. She let the impact of her question sink in for a second or two.

"Get the craziness out of your system today and then tomorrow get it together. Jonas needs you as a father right now. I sense from the way Simon was speaking and how you are now, that you might not be able to 'fix' this. If you can, great. If not, be the father your boy needs."

Jonas was struggling. He had a drink problem before the accident. Money had never been an issue as his parents provided an allowance that was more than lots of people earned in a 9 to 5 job. There was nothing to save for as he was given cars for birthday presents and when he needed a home of his own, that would be gifted to him as well. He had cash and he had time on his hands. He ran the odd errand for his dad, but other than that he did what he liked. He was soon befriended in the local bars by those who knew he had the funds to keep their glasses topped up, and in return they made sure he had lots of fun. His new 'mates' were always game for a laugh and girls seemed to find bad boys attractive, so getting laid was never a problem.

After the accident, he had struggled to cope. His dad and the lawyer had worked wonders in getting such a small sentence, but he still had to do his time. His own predicament had suppressed any feelings of remorse leading up to, and during, the trial, but once he was locked up he had plenty of time to just think. He was so canned up at the time he hit that lad, that he had struggled to recall very much. Now, however, either his subconscious was leaking him bits of information here and there, or his mind was making things up. Either way, the film in his mind of Tobias, as the car struck him, had become extremely vivid. The muffled thump of metal on flesh and bone, the forever haunting shock of eyes and the slow motion of his body being projected, cartwheeling through the air. With every repeat more details were added, punishing him, torturing him and most painful of all, reminding him of that fateful day, again and again.

Being a rich boy in prison, meant protection in return for certain favours. So, he bought drugs for those who could keep the thugs and rapists at bay and then as a coping mechanism he dabbled himself. The relief was glorious, the subsequent addiction excruciating and the longer-term effects on his mental health began to emerge.

Once out, his parents saw the change his sentence had bestowed upon him. They had been worried about his drinking, but he was a young lad and many needed to get the lure of alcohol out of their system. At least to a point where it was no longer the master. This was different. Physically, he was a bag of bones, slumbering about and rarely looking up. When he did, his sparkling, youthful eyes, had aged and yellowed and dimmed. If that was not enough, mentally he was shot. He had once been confident, outgoing and willing to take on anything. To see such a positive outlook on life replaced with a sullen, frightened shadow of his former self, was agonising for them. He had two major displays of real emotion. Temper, raging temper when he needed a fix, and outbursts of sobbing, which could occur anytime he was not high. Prison was his sentence, guilt was his punishment.

They paid for rehab. He stayed off drink and drugs for a while, but without them his life was a void. So, he drifted back. Intoxicated by the temptations of a mistress who promised to block everything out, save for the buzz of the hit. Problem was, the pleasure he had once associated with his pills and syringes, had been overtaken by nothing more than relief. He no longer needed to have a sensation of soaring on high, his addiction was to any substance that could offer the respite of being numbed to life. The ease with which any strand of narcotics could be obtained was incredible. It shocked Reg and Carla. They paid for the second stint of rehab when dealers began arriving on the property to sell their wares. This time there were conditions. Either he left the drink and drugs alone or his allowance would stop. At the rehab centre one of the counsellors requested a chat with them. It was time for some tough love and it was a difficult message for them to take. No blame game, just a realisation they may have contributed to him being how he is. That was in the past, far more crucial right now, was to think very carefully about how they could best support Jonas to shake this dependence on drugs. Reg immediately took offence and became irate. How dare they blame them, they were terrific parents. Carla asked the counsellor for five minutes with her husband. He had paced the room and was staring out of the window. Looking at nothing in particular, just staring. She placed her hands around his waist and squeezed.

"If you want our son to get better, then we have to listen to the experts. It doesn't matter how he ended up like this, all that matters is we get our Jonas back."

As his wife's gentle voice sounded out his son's name, he welled up. His emotions were already high, so her lightest of touch had merely redirected them. She felt the tension begin to dissolve, he took a sustained intake of air and released a huge sigh. She knew him well enough to know he was fighting to keep the tears at bay.

"We have spoiled our son. He has had everything too easy and it's time we tried a different way. He has so much time on his hands and as the counsellor said, that is thinking time. He needs a job, something to focus his thoughts on and we can easily sort that. It wasn't an attack on us. It was making us face up to what we need to do."

She pulled him round to face her. This time her soft tone was more forceful.

"I am finishing the session with that counsellor. It's up to you if you chose to or not, but if you do come back in, you listen to what is being said without any more histrionics."

Then she smiled at him.

"I could do with my man beside me."

With the counsellor facilitating the discussion, Jonas agreed a plan with his parents. He would join a support group and this time attend at least weekly. He would go through his phone and delete all the dealers and hangers on. Then he would get a job. But what? He had never had to consider what he wanted to do. Some jobs were best discounted, such as anything that brought him into contact with alcohol, for the temptation, or cars, for the resurrection of ghosts of the past. Reg had a mate in property development, so until they found something to sustain for the long term, Jonas could labour for him. It was physical work, long hours with travelling involved and hopefully a sense of achievement to be part of turning neglected properties into beautiful homes ready to sell.

It had worked well. Jonas had begun to redevelop some of his old personality and he enjoyed the feel of muscles the work had prospered. He was fit, spending his time productively and with some encouragement from his dad, he had begun to consider buying properties to develop on his own.

So why had this descended on them now just as things were looking up for Jonas? Reg was totally engrossed with how the trial could be prevented and so preoccupied that all other considerations were lost on him. Carla was thinking about the practicalities of the position they would be put in. Jonas would have to stay away from work and that meant more of that agonizing time to think, reflect and remember. If that was not enough, all the family would need to cut themselves off from the main stream news channels and of course social media. She knew some publicity seeking idiot would say the death penalty was no more than her boy deserved. In fact, this was a launch pad for all those people who wanted capital punishment restored and this case would be a prime vehicle to drive their argument forward. The first trial had been unbearable, with all the things that were said about Jonas and the family. This time the vitriol would be at fever pitch.

Jonas was already showing signs of breaking down. Reg was acting tough, but such was the fervent state of every emotion he lived through, he could crack if things didn't go his way. Carla had to be strong. Things had been tough before, but the life of her son was being threatened and chances were her family was on the brink of becoming pariahs again.

CHAPTER 26.

The third degree;
To question someone intensely or forcefully.
The expression derives either from the criminal justice code, when illustrating
the various degrees of murder, or from the Freemasons, an all-male
fellowship which holds extravagant secret ceremonies, and whose members,
in order to become "third degree members" or "Master Masons", have to
undergo vigorous questioning.

At 2pm exactly, the Speaker of the House of Commons stood to his feet and an expectant hush devoured every sound in the chamber. He simply said, *The Prime Minister.* Peter Manger was used to all eyes being on him at the despatch box, but he felt some of the old nerves his more inexperienced self would have encountered. He delivered a modified version of what he had said in Cabinet Office Briefing Room A to brief the members of the house. Then he laid out what would happen.

Jonas Rafferty will stand trial again for the homicide of Tobias Langley. By definition, the offence cannot be termed 'murder', however the prosecution legal team are claiming 'intent' can be pursued. It is their view, the act of being so under the influence of alcohol was akin to planning a killing. The judge, Gareth Peters-Hampton, will make a ruling on this ahead of the trial commencing. That said, to be absolutely clear, in accordance with the demands being placed upon them, the death penalty is to be an available sentence for the judge. The trial would begin in two days' time. Once he had concluded his statement, he would ask the leader of the opposition to respond. Beyond that, there was to be no further discussion and no opportunity to ask questions. He accepted this would be unpopular, but what would be the point? There was no space to ask local party members and constituents for their views. Both of the main party leaders, senior members of the government and other senior figures from the police and military had agreed on the way forward.

Arguing about principles of law and ethics was a luxury 5 million people did not have. In due course the honourable members would thank him, because the burden of conscience was being carried by a few and it was extremely heavy.

There is likely to be a high demand for the removal of Chipsules, but these will only be extracted for medical reasons, requiring the authority of a GP and a senior person in the local health trust. At each revelation there was a collective gasp and raised voices. He spoke over them to continue. This pattern continued at each successive point. Once he had stated there would be no debate on the matter, there was total uproar. Peter Manger finished his brief and sat down without even turning round. The speaker rose and demanded order. He was to demand it several times before any semblance of calm returned. Once he was sufficiently content with the level of noise, he called on Phyllis Stoppard to speak.

"Thank you Mr Speaker. Along with a few others I have been privy to the details of the situation and I would like to thank the Prime Minister for involving me, as the representative of this side of the house. What he demonstrated through his action is that this is beyond party politics. To those of any and all political persuasion, I would urge a word of caution. Your immediate reaction, based on whatever ethics, principles or values you personally hold, is unlikely to remain constant. I have shifted position many times and to be true, I am still uncertain about the path I have chosen. On one side we have a young man, who felt he had served his time, repaid his debt to society and was attempting to move on with his life. He did, however, take a life through being reckless at the hands of a powerful vehicle. Call it manslaughter or murder, many felt his sentence was lenient at the original trial. Then we have a mother, not only suffering the intolerable pain of losing her son, but then feeling being totally let down by the justice of this land. Whilst we all move on to the next, latest news headline, she cannot. Do I agree with her actions in this matter? Of course not. Do I have an understanding of why she felt this was necessary? Yes. Take your time honourable members. Be it one or five million, there is at least one life at stake and that demands your best thinking. Do not be rushed or risk being trapped forever by an immediate, hasty, coming to of a conclusion. Mark my words, once this trial is over, your declarations on this matter will follow you for your career. Be considered in opinions, as opposed to opinionated in your considerations. After all that has been said, I do not know if I'm doing the right thing, but there is no right or wrong, there is only the best decision we can make on the evidence and information in front of us. To that end, the Prime Minister has my unwavering support in the choice being made. There is no benefit that I can see through a debate. The trial is happening. Finally, can we and everyone throughout the land, spare a thought for the Langley family and the Rafferty family. God knows what they are going through."

As she sat back down, Peter Manger rose to his feet and nodded his head purposefully in the direction of Phyllis Stoppard and the unusual sound of a ripple of applause tiptoed its way around those old benches. Most seemed unsure whether to join in or not, so the clapping was genuine, if not unanimous. Then the Prime Minister exited the chamber.

He knew he was walking straight into the onslaught of the TV crews and journalists, but he was calm as he had already laid the foundations for how this would be presented. He would happily give interviews, but there was to be no sensationalism in the reporting. If there was, he would refuse any further requests for interviews on this topic from the culprits and in the future on other topics from those same offenders. He demanded no scaremongering about the Chipsules. During his conversations with the media heavyweights he had provided the specific example of, any channel using one of their listed experts to deliver an explanation on how they could be used to release poison into the human system. They were to report the news, not to try and create their own. Get your boys and girls in line or he would use his position to name names of rogue reporters and companies who risked lives of every day citizens; those same citizens who paid their wages in some way shape or form. The tail was not wagging this dog in these circumstances.

He left the building and was heading for his official car when a number of questions were flung his way. Above them all he heard this.

"How many of the 5 million people carrying a Chipsule are at risk of dying from poisoning Prime Minister?"

His head was just about to duck into the vehicle, but he stopped and looked to see if he could make out who had said it. There was a young man, in his twenties probably, waving a small microphone in his general direction and looking quite pleased with himself. He was amongst a small group of journalists, all of whom were well acquainted with hurling such questions at senior politicians and rarely expecting to get a response. Peter Manger looked about and spotted what he was looking for, a TV camera and it was pointed straight at him. He strode towards the man who had asked the question.

"Can I ask which organisation you represent?"

"The Chronicle."

An instant reply, delivered with the same pride the young man assumed his editor was feeling at this precise moment.

"Thank you. The owner of your newspaper has assured me there will be no ill-thought out questions asked regarding this whole situation as we all accept it is far too important for any such puerile stupidity. So, with the whole world watching, can you explain how you feel such a question is of value to your readers?"

Pride was replaced with incredulity. Most hacks had been through the ringer enough to not feel embarrassment any more, but not many had been fronted up by the Prime Minister live on TV.

"I thought not." Peter Manger said, once the silence had established no good answer was coming his way anytime soon. "Unless I get a full apology from your owner and editor for your crass attempt at creating a headline, your newspaper will not be party to any interviews my ministers or myself give on this matter and will be barred from briefings at No 10. Have a good day everyone."

Yes, it was harsh, but he wanted to lay it out straight away that the normal jousting between politicians and reporters was suspended whilst the trial was going on. He had expected some hound to cross the line and his retort was a gamble. He assumed the editor of the Chronicle was now phoning his fellow editors to discuss the freedom of the press to ask questions, how they felt about the threat of being excluded from interviews/briefings and if he made a stand, were they with him? His hope was that they would say, do you mean you want us to give up the hottest ticket in town, because some gobby journo of yours overstepped his mark? It might blow up in his face, but as he had spoken to the main players and shakers already, he doubted it.

His personal security copper was beside him.

"Do you think I went OTT with that lad?"

"No sir. He did an inflammatory piece about what he called 'the incompetence of the British bobby' a while back. Gets everything he deserves in my book and I hope there is plenty more crap heading his way."

* * *

Eloise Langley watched the speech from her cell. Graeme had been very kind and gave his permission that she could retain the use of her tablet, once he had checked with his technical boys and girls that no 'app' was installed that could make contact with the Chipsules. Her door was pushed to, as opposed to locked, and the custody team were briefed to be generous with her exercise time in the courtyard. Why was he so trusting? Well, as she had pointed out, she had her trial and she had the sentencing penalty for the trial she had insisted on. Why would she do anything silly now?

Prior to the screening, a Simon Burgess, legal representative for the Rafferty family, had been in touch. Not directly, but he had spoken to the custody sergeant, and asked him to relay a message. Carla Rafferty wanted to know if they could talk; mother to mother. Eloise knew the point of the conversation would be to pull at her heart strings and try to find a way forward that did not risk the life of her son. She declined the request. Her reply was to the effect that Jonas had made choices that killed her son and that Reginald had shown scant regard for her feelings as a mother at the last trial. She added, if he had let justice take its course first time around, this situation may never had arisen.

Graeme King felt letting her retain control of her phone was a step too far and would smack of gross favouritism, but as she had agreed to stay beyond the normal time he was allowed to hold her in custody voluntarily, the tablet did not seem unreasonable. She agreed someone at the station would monitor her messages, as that meant she could keep in touch with Andrew and Alana via messenger. Words With Friends wiled away many hours and also helped her remain feeling connected to those she was playing.

* * *

Simon Burgess was in his office looking through some case papers when his secretary knocked on his door and walked in. She had the Home Office waiting on the line for him. He picked up the phone and introduced himself.

"Please hold for the Home Secretary."

The Home Secretary calling him could only be about one thing. He was not kept waiting for any length of time at all.

"Hello Mr Burgess."

"Good morning Home Secretary."

"Sorry to have kept you and my apologies for calling you out of the blue, but I felt we needed to discuss the Rafferty case."

"I assumed as much."

"Good. This call will be a one off as I realise how out of the norm it is, but in all honesty, what isn't about this case? You will be doing your job and seeking ways to delay this case coming to court and considering all manner of appeals to prevent it going ahead, so it is only fair you know I will use my powers to prevent any such appeal being heard ahead of the trial. I will use those same powers to refute any attempts to cause a delay in the trial starting. I do not do either of these things lightly, but you have one client to represent, whereas I have a nation. Could I be any clearer?"

"I think you have made your point. Similar messages were conveyed to me by your Home Office officials when I was first contacted about the trial, but not quite in such robust terms. Of course, you are preventing me from doing my job and I have to make my client aware of that and to petition wider interested parties for their support in preventing you from, quite frankly, riding roughshod over the law of the land."

"Now you see why it was more expedient for us to talk. As of when the PM finished speaking in Parliament, the case was subject to sub judice. So it cannot be discussed in the House and any 'parties', as you call them, will be under no illusion as to how serious we will consider their actions if they try to interfere with proceedings. All major media outlets know what is expected of them and we will make everyone aware of how we will pursue charges of contempt of court if they cross the line."

"I thought we had a free press."

"We do Mr Burgess, absolutely we do. It is your right to see what support you can muster in whatever way you see fit and it is their right to decide whether to run with it. My advice to you, is to focus your efforts on the trial itself as I cannot see any way of it not going ahead on the due date. I have no desire for Jonas to be sentenced to death, because whether you believe it or not, I follow the law of the land and we do not have capital punishment. My call is intended as an indication of how you can best spend your time in representing young Mr Rafferty. Thank you."

Once the call had ended, Simon Burgess felt deflated. His tried and tested strategy of many years was in tatters. The trial was imminent and he realised he could huff and puff, but his chances of preventing the hearing were no more than minimal. He had been clinging onto some hope of causing a delay, at least, but having spoken to the Home Secretary, it was clear any optimism, minor though it was, had been misplaced. The government were playing hardball with the press and did he really have anything to offer them that would risk their alienation from the inner goings on of the case? Probably not. There would be no technicalities to seek this time either. He needed to dig very deep into the previous trial papers, to review all the witness statements and find the best way to prevent the ultimate penalty being bestowed on Jonas. Guilty was a foregone conclusion, so what was the best way to prevent the loss of life. What felt like a victory at the last trial, could soon turn into a tragic loss.

Jonas was clearly his major concern, but without doubt he knew his own reputation was at stake here. His defence at the first trial would come under scrutiny again and if Jonas was sentenced to death, the only time it would be used possibly ever again, would that be his professional legacy? Like every other practising lawyer in this country, he had no experience in presenting a case to request leniency from the judge, against execution of his client. He needed to get up to speed quickly. Then it dawned on him exactly what the Home Secretary had said to him during their call. Do not waste time on matters where there was no likelihood of a good conclusion. Instead, prepare for a trial, the likes of which he had never been involved in before and would never be again. The best outcome for everyone, apart from Eloise Langley perhaps, was a guilty verdict and custodial sentence, of which Jonas had already spent some time. Certainly Joy Hamilton knew there was no victory for the government in this; damage limitation was the extent of her ambition.

CHAPTER 27.

No spring chicken;
A person who is no longer young.
Chicks need to be raised in light, warm conditions, and in the past, it was not
possible to create these special conditions like we do nowadays, so it was not
possible for chicks to be raised in the winter. Farmers soon realised that
chickens born in the spring were the most desirable at markets and buyers
would pay the most for them. Farmers would often try to sell an older chicken
pretending that it was born in the spring, but smart buyers would say, "that's
no spring chicken!"

The Rafferty household was coming under extreme pressure and their long marriage
was showing signs of breaking down. Following the rebuffal from Eloise Langley to
meet, and the reasons given for this, Carla accused Reg of stupid arrogance for the
way he had acted with Eloise at the first trial. She was only too aware it was not his
style to be a passive winner and he had ruffled many feathers in both his personal
and professional dealings because of this. But, if he had not been so loud and proud
then, this would not be happening. Their son had been pronounced guilty of
manslaughter and whilst she was pleased with the moderation of the time he would
serve in prison, she knew this was not something to shout about. Perhaps she had
been in his shadow for too long, accepting the comfortable life on offer and not
questioning the methods enough. If he did not want things on a more equal footing,
then perhaps, just perhaps, it was time for her to find someone who did.
Reginald Rafferty had built a comfortable life for his family and his methods had
never been questioned by his wife before. Well, not really. So how come he was to
blame for all of this now? She had not been so strong in her condemnation at the
time and had never requested restraint on his behalf. He had paid a lot of money to
have Mr Burgess represent Jonas and based on the outcome it was money well spent.
He knew his wealth was an attractive commodity for a certain type of woman and if

he was not appreciated by Carla anymore, there would be others who he was sure would welcome his advances.

On top of their relationship issues, Simon Burgess had personally called on them and explained there was no real hope of the trial being delayed and certainly not cancelled. He, needed to work on the defence and they, needed to show a united front. He could sense the strain they were under, but he had a request. When the trial began they should arrive together, leave together, hold hands wherever possible and generally show what a happy couple they were. The jury and the public would have fashioned a view on the Rafferty family through what was, and had been, reported, so the solidity of their marriage and family unit was vital in shaping the image they needed to best support Jonas.

The police had arrived and taken Jonas into custody. All done professionally, but was there really a need for a squad car, three burly coppers and handcuffs? He was to stand trial for manslaughter again, so he would be held at a local police station in the meantime. It was devastating. Carla cried at the time and at any given minute, for no particular reason, she could burst into more tears. Reg was all over the place. He was angry, he had no control over what was happening and if he admitted it, most of all he was scared. He loved Carla and he loved Jonas and he was in very serious danger of losing them both. His money was a worthless currency all of a sudden and, with that, his usual influence had disappeared. It hurt. He was emasculated at the very time he needed to be strong. As he had removed himself from his business interests for the time being he had plenty of time for contemplation. As his mind was allowed to run free it began to produce attacks on his self-identity and the approach to life it spawned. The most devastating thought proved to be wondering if this was karma. Was his son's life at risk, because of how he had treated people? In ways, the speed of the trial beginning was a blessing he had not considered, because if it had been dragged out for too long, his very sanity could have been at risk.

CHAPTER 28.

Acid test;
A sure test, giving an incontestable result.
Gold prospectors and dealers need to be able to distinguish gold from base
metal. The original acid test was developed in the late 18th century and relied
on nitric acid's ability to dissolve other metals more readily than gold. To
confirm that a find was gold it was given 'the acid test'.

It was here. The day of the trial.

Reginald Rafferty was wearing a black, two piece suit, white shirt and dark patterned tie. His tan shoes were highly polished. Carla was wearing a dark blue dress, matching shoes and expensive, but modest in appearance, jewellery of a necklace and bracelet to accompany the only ring she wore, her wedding band. He commented on how nice she looked and she made a last minute adjustment to his tie. They kissed, just a peck, but somehow it made both feel better, stronger. As instructed by Simon, but actually without need for such an instruction as it happened, they held hands and left their house. A trusted employee of Reg's was waiting to take them to the courthouse and that would be this person's only job for as long as the trial lasted.

Eloise would travel in a police van. She wore exactly the same clothes as she had for the first trial. The grey & white checked, one piece dress, red jacket and coordinating shoes had not been worn at all since she took them off having returned home from hearing the sentence passed down to Jonas. As a statement it said, she had not moved on. It said, she was picking up from the point where the Rafferty's, and their legal team, had introduced the technicality that was to totally change the direction the trial had been taking. Her choice of clothes might be noticed by Jonas or his parents or they might not. She did not much care, they were hugely symbolic to her. Graeme King tried his best, but he never really scrubbed up any better than, crumpled. He would do his top shirt button up and have his tie as tight to the collar as possible, but beyond that his other major contribution to looking smart, would be to rub his shoes on the back of his trousers before entering court. He had a certain liking for Eloise and he could empathise with her to a certain extent, but he was not sure if he would ever agree with her choice of action. His job today was to accompany Eloise in the police van and be prepared to give evidence if called. Not difficult really, as he had provided evidence in front of a judge on many occasions, but the significance of today's proceedings was not lost on him. With that came a few extra nerves. His wife had asked if he wanted to wear his cufflinks. No. Why attract attention by being flashy. She grinned at her man and repeated 'flashy', whilst grinning and shaking her head. Surprise Christmas presents get more difficult to buy as you age and her choice of shirt jewellery for him last year might as well have remained unwrapped.

Peter Manger and Joy Hamilton had busy days so would not be able to watch the trial live, but both had made arrangements to be kept up to date with the proceedings. They had an agreement that if anything substantial happened they would immediately take a call from each other. They would communicate exactly that to whoever they would be in the company of. The trial could not end soon enough for them and whilst the speed of its commencement was begrudgingly enforced on them, now that it was happening, they were secretly quite pleased.

Judge Gareth Peters-Hamilton was in his element. He had given up public office not so long ago to spend more time with his wife, children and grandchildren, but the truth was he had ended up with far too much time on his hands. His wife had her own interests, developed over many years, and the rest of the family had lives of their own. He did see them more than he had, but the level of sheer boredom had taken him by surprise. The call, requesting he preside in this most unusual case, could not have been more welcome. Albeit for a short time, he would have a purpose, something to spring out of bed for, if his aging bones let him spring. He would be, Your Honour, again. The thought of having capital punishment available to him as a sentence, had not really affected the way he prepared for the case. He had sent bad men to prison for life and made it clear he meant life. Was a life incarcerated, in other words a life without liberty, so different to not being alive? Everything was happening remarkably quickly to the normal speed of legal proceedings, so he had to get used to being back in the saddle with utmost urgency. There was no guidance available on when a death sentence should be passed, and any previous guidance was so outdated it had no use for the current day. The senior Civil Servant at the Home Office had been very clear. Hear the case. Decide whether guilty or not and then, if necessary, a panel would be assembled to assist him in deciding the penalty. Joy Hamilton, as Home Secretary, would Chair such a panel and would be joined by a number of top judges. It was also made clear there would be no fudging on the sentencing. Whatever was deemed appropriate would be passed down. Eloise Langley would sniff out any attempted dereliction of duty and the possible response to that was unthinkable.

Peter Manger and Joy Hamilton were anxious about how the case would go and the eventual outcome. DCI Graeme King was just wanting the trial to be over. His life was better when he was in his own station, chasing down baddies. Being trucked up in a suit & tie in a courtroom was not his comfort zone. Simon Burgess had been up late last night with several of his legal practice team around him. He was driving them really hard, as they had little time to prepare for one of the highest profile cases he, or anyone else actually, would be party to. The stress was showing as he shouted and ranted at them. Judge Peters-Hamilton was happy in his work.

Jonas sat in his cell awaiting his transport. He was in a skinny style, grey suit and thin grey tie over a white shirt. His shoes were black. The isolation and loneliness of being in four plain walls, with little human interaction, allows the mind to wander freely and, as he knew only too well, often it seeks out dark places. There was the odd break for meals, the duty officer opening the flap to make sure he was okay and visits from his solicitor. In the meantime, he reflected on the accident, which for a long while had been a blur due to the synthetic substances he had invited to invade his body and influence his mind. As time passed the haziness had gradually cleared, but it was unlikely if he would ever know if he was recollecting the actual event or visioning it, based on what people had told him from the witness statements. However, Jonas remembered with extreme clarity what prison was like. The drugs may have affected some parts of his memory, but they could not block out the experience. The prospect of going back was causing even more turmoil inside his dilapidated head. It was tortuous to try and reconcile how it could be that, after being wild for so long, and just when it seemed he was getting things together, he should be subjected to all of this now. Life had no rhyme or reason, life could be cruel. If ever he could do with the crutch of a drug or hit of alcohol it was at this precise moment. Then the loop began again and he saw the face of Tobias Langley. It was an image that had been shown in lots of the papers when he had gone through this process previously and was now being displayed all over again. Jonas sat very still in his cell as his demons went to work. He was crying.

CHAPTER 29.

Saved by the bell;
Saved by a last minute intervention.
The expression is boxing slang and it came into being in the latter half of the
19th century. A boxer who is in danger of losing a bout can be 'saved' from
defeat by the respite signalled by bell that marks the end of a round.

The trial was to start at 10am. At 8.45am exactly, DCI Graeme King received a call from the Duty Sergeant to say Eloise Langley needed to speak with him urgently. He left the rest of the emails he had been working through and hurried down to see her. When he arrived, he was expecting her to be in a state of panic or distress of some kind, but she was her normal, calm, composed self. Sitting, hands in lap, she smiled without parting her lips and gently patted the seat next to her for him to sit down. His tilted head, half squinting eyes and furrowed brow, let loose his puzzlement. He sat down. Eloise picked up her tablet.

"Graeme, what I am about to show you will be released through my YouTube channel at 9.45am. I'm not sure what will happen to me once it has been seen by your bosses, so before you watch it, I wanted to say thank you. You are a fabulous police officer, honest as the day is long and principled to the extreme. Also, you have the makings of a pretty decent human being from what I've seen. Ready?"

"That's nice of you to say, thank you. That said, you are making me very nervous Eloise, what's going on?"

"Watch and see." Her face was exhibiting excitement. Such is the lack of trust in human nature a police officer develops through their work, his immediate thought was that she would be providing evidence of the lethal power of her Chipsules. But why? She had no reason to do that as far as he knew.

She pressed a few buttons on the screen keyboard, which he assumed were a code to access the content. Then, on the screen, was Eloise. She looked nice. Her black blouse contrasted with the plain, cream background and she stared at the camera.

"I am making this recording on the day I will hand myself into the police. My intention is to publicise the failings of our justice system and to do this I will take some very extreme measures that may upset people to a lesser or greater degree. However, I am not taking these actions with any considerations for my popularity."

With the camera still running she reached forward, lifted a glass of water and sipped. For dramatic effect or to steady herself, Graeme King wondered.

"My son Tobias was killed by Jonas Rafferty in a car accident. At the time Mr Rafferty was heavily under the influence of drink; he should not have been in control of any sort of vehicle, let alone a fast, powerful car. He was speeding. The actions he took on that day robbed me of my son."

Her voice broke slightly, but she looked down briefly and regained some control.

"His parents, mostly his father I believe, decided on their own course of action. They threw money at the system. They used their ample resources to secure top legal representation and whatever influence their grubby wealth could obtain. The result went their way. Jonas was guilty, but whilst I was never to see my son again, Jonas would be free to walk the streets in a couple of years. Not only was I robbed of my son, but I was cheated out of justice. I could not, cannot, and will not, accept that money should buy exclusion from justice. In part or in full."

The camera was still, but even without zooming in, it was clear there were tears in her eyes. Anger, frustration, perhaps a little of both, were causing her to water up.

"This video will only be released into the public arena if I have achieved what I set out to do. To anyone watching this, it will be clear what I have done. I have held the government, the legal and judicial systems to ransom. I can never apologise enough for any distress I have caused. In time, if not now, I hope at least some of you can understand what prompted such a choice on my behalf. My methods have been extreme, but the outcome is that I am on the verge of justice, finally. Jonas Rafferty is awaiting trial. The money that spared him his true penalty last time is ineffective now. Everyone who knew Tobias, felt a great loss at his untimely and brutal passing. Those who know Jonas Rafferty cannot have prevented themselves from considering the 'what if' of this trial. Through the realisation that he may be taken from them, they are experiencing a tiny piece of what my family, and the friends of Tobias, have lived through."

On screen she bowed her head, ran both hands through her hair and then stared deep into the lens. Graeme looked up from the screen at Eloise, but she was locked onto that tablet.

"However, there will be no trial. I am a health professional and my ethics, my values, my very being, is about saving lives, not taking them. The truth is, there is no poison in any Chipsule. There is no danger to anyone who has them implanted. On the contrary they continue to support a healthier life. With that admission, my leverage has vanished."

Eloise looked up from the tablet and mouthed at Graeme, 'I told you your family were not at risk'. Then she returned her gaze to the tablet.

"Heaven only knows what will happen to me now, it doesn't really matter. What does matter to me, is that there is now a public debate on what justice should look, feel and yes even taste like, going forward. I have a certain amount of fame, I have access to key individuals in our nation, including senior politicians, and I have a sizeable fortune in comparison to most people. If justice can be manipulated around me, then think what will happen should a loved one of yours become a victim. If they come up against a rich boy or girl, then seriously, what are your chances for true justice?"

From somewhere out of camera she reached out and produced a photo of Tobias, which she held up next to her face.

"I will not get justice for Tobias. I have failed him. I am certainly not the only person who feels let down by our system and I will not be the last if things do not change. Do you want to be a statistic? Do you want to be a victim? Or do you want to know that, should the situation arise, your loved one will be treated fairly and shown the respect they deserve. Tobias was shown no respect. He was nothing more than a name and warranted nothing more than a shrug of the shoulders at his lack of justice. Is that what you want? Then contact your local MP, sign any and every petition that supports a change in our warped judicial system. Right now, is the time to be brave. Right now, is the time to stand up and be counted. Right now, is the time to be an advocate of that change. Or......take your chance on being a victim; a silent victim regretting your passivity. Thank you."

As the on-screen Eloise was replaced by a close up of Tobias for a few seconds, which then disappeared into a black dot on the screen, the Eloise next to Graeme King closed the tablet case and turned to him.

"Well, you'd better run along and tell the boys and girls up the line what you've just seen and heard. Then I'd like to know what will happen to me."

She reached over and squeezed his hand. Big smile this time and then she let go. He was still taking it all in, but the release of her grip sparked him into life and he hastily left the cell. As he headed through the custody desk area he asked one of the officers there to get Eloise a tea, because *I think she might need it.*

CHAPTER 30.

Cat got your tongue;
A question addressed to someone who is silent.
The phrase is just an example of the light-hearted imagery that is, or was,
directed at children.

Graeme King made two calls as soon as he reached his office. The first was to Joy Hamilton and the second to Superintendent Jeremy Day. The first call was obvious, the second was sensible. It looked like he would survive unscathed from this massive, potential, banana skin, so to then mess it up by not keeping his boss up to speed would just be silly. Status and internal politics were not his forte, but pain avoidance was, and if Jeremy Day had not heard it from him immediately, the grief would be long and excruciating. He called DI Rebecca Blades in and told her what was happening, and then called the whole squad together for an impromptu update. Some were annoyed at the waste of police time, others just relieved it was done and dusted, but most saw the big picture. They thought about the threat that had been lifted from everyone they knew who had a Chipsule fitted. It did not matter if there had never actually been a cause for concern. The menace had felt very real. Equally real, was the relief at this news.

Joy Hamilton had worked into the early hours of the morning on the contents of her ministerial 'Red Box'. She was in the process of distributing the work that needed to follow on from her actioning them, when she received the call from DCI King. The relief she felt was immense. The chances of a death penalty being issued for a drunk driving incident were not large, but the scrutiny of their actions as a government, the trial even being on again and the riding roughshod over laid down laws were likely to be remembered by political commentators, and in turn members of the public, long into the future. She immediately picked up her phone to relay the news to Peter Manger. He saw who was calling and answered straightaway, then had to cut short her zealous offloading of information, whilst he found a more private spot.

His relief was intense. As it sunk in, the physical manifestation of what he was feeling was teetering between laughing and crying. He was still bristling from the way his niece had been involved, but thank heavens things could get back to their normal level. Every day as Prime Minister was frantic enough, but mostly child's play in comparison.

DCI King had opened up the topic on what exactly to do with Eloise now. There were obvious charges that could be brought against her, such as wasting police time for one, but he was looking for a steer on how tough his approach was to be. His personal view was to always play it by the book, but he also knew there were occasions when 'examples' needed to be made of individuals for certain crimes. He was enquiring, was this such an occasion? Joy put forward her view to deal with it in exactly the same way he would any other person in his charge. When she spoke to the PM, she told him what her advice had been; he concurred. Petty vendettas were not their style.

Simon Burgess was informed by a member of his back up team, following a telephone call from the Home Office. Half disbelieving, he checked out the news with a member of the prosecution and was given a short nod of concurrence. He immediately went to find Reginald & Carla Rafferty, who he had left on some seats a while earlier. They embraced. A loving embrace. All was good in the world again. Reg bearhugged Simon, lifting him completely off the floor and twirling him round and round. Delighted as he was, for Simon this was all a little too macho for his liking and certainly not the done thing inside a court building. Once Reg plonked him back on solid ground, he led the Rafferty's to find Jonas. He felt the news might be best coming from mum and dad.

Jonas looked up as the door opened, expecting it be a police officer to escort him to the dock. Instead, he saw two huge, beaming smiles as his parents entered. Reginald did the talking.

"Jonas, it's over. There isn't going to be a trial, we're taking you home right now. You're free Jonas, do you understand?"

Then he lifted his son off the seat he was perched on and hugged him. However, his boy was limp, he did not even hug his dad back. Carla put her hand on his cheek. Then Jonas wept. Openly. Loudly. The outpouring was pure, visceral, emotion. It was uncontrollable and to his dad it was uncomfortable. But Carla knew it was necessary. She pulled Reg off her son and then held him in her arms. It was as if he had regressed to a child as he rested his head on her shoulder and wailed and blubbed. A mother's instinct told her he needed to get this out of his core, his innermost subconscious, as it had been bubbling away for who knew how long. She made the sympathetic, encouraging noises that reassured him this was alright. Everything, was alright.

CHAPTER 31.

Push the envelope;
Go beyond commonly accepted boundaries.
The term "pushing the envelope" originally comes from the field of aviation. It
is a reference to the flyable portion of the atmosphere that envelopes the earth.
Pilots would push the envelope when they were testing the speed or elevation
limits of new aircraft.

Eloise was deep in contemplation. They had achieved all they hoped to. Sure, there
would be a bit more to come her way in terms of 'punishment' for what she had
done, but unless she had read things completely wrong it would be a fine and a
warning. No big deal. The authorities might have some suspicions, but as it stood
they were only interested in her for what had happened. That was how she wanted it
to stay. Bob may have been the joint architect of this whole plan, but that would go
with her to the grave. He was on a Yacht somewhere, monitoring his laptop. He had
alerted Eloise to John Kuria's indiscretion, he had supplied the material on the PM's
niece and provided the details on those patients who had the Chipsules implanted.
The tablet Eloise kept with her at all times was encrypted in such a way, that simple
monitoring techniques would not find the channel they used to pass through such
information. If it had been taken away from her, he would simply have provided the
same evidence through journalists, but Plan A was always their preference.
She missed him terribly. Alana, lovely, innocent, was with him. She was missing her
so much too. How great would it be to have all the family together again? Well, no
Tobias of course, but he would be the honorary guest; in spirit. Could it be called a
celebration when they had not changed anything? To others, perhaps not. To them,
it definitely was. A discussion, a meaningful exploration into the legal system was
growing support and combined voices across the population were demanding to be
heard. The method may have been extreme, but if not their words, their efforts, their
pain would have been given masked sympathetic platitudes and then...and

then...nothing. Right now, they had the authorities' attention. That was already a 'win'.

It was quite some time before Graeme King returned to see Eloise. The paper cup on the floor near the bed she was sitting on told him his request for a tea had been met. She saw where his eyes were looking.

"Did you arrange that? Thank you." Then she pulled a 'yuk' face. He grinned.

"You asked earlier what would happen to you, so how about we discuss that?"

"Yes please."

"I will be looking to charge you...."

"What with?"

"Eloise, seriously? You have threatened the lives of 5 million people and...."

"I most certainly have not. At worst I inferred a claim or two about what my Chipsules could do and provided the number of people who had been implanted."

"OK then, you implied a threat."

"Did I? Perhaps you interpreted my words incorrectly."

"What about the Prime Minister's niece, are you saying that wasn't a threat?"

"If you think back, you will find I provided factual information about Miss Parker, most of which I gained from an internet search, I should add, and you put two and two together. There was no specific threat."

"What about Harry Vaughen?"

"Died of natural causes. I always said I 'might' be responsible, but of course I never was. His death was timely for my purpose, that's all. It could have been someone else, if they had passed away at the right time."

"What about the distress you caused his family through your claim. Hardly sensitive was it?"

"I figured you police guys would not rush into revealing too much to his family and by the time you felt you had to, I would have put everything to rest anyway."

"Just so I can gauge how things will transpire from here on in, are you of the opinion that having claimed you could be responsible for a murder, indicating you have the means & method to carry out 5 million or so more murders, having delivered what sounded like a thinly veiled threat on the niece of the standing Prime Minister and countless ancillary crimes, do you think you will walk away scot free?"

"Of course not. I have chosen my words very carefully throughout this whole situation, however you and the others on your side have chosen to translate them is up to you, and up to them. I accept I will have to face my comeuppance for taking so much of your time, and that of some other officers, but beyond that I think you will do well to tread carefully once my legal team are let loose."

"Wow!"

"I haven't finished yet. I have made my point and achieved all I wanted to, so it is up to others to decide if they want to take the baton on. I want nothing more than to get back to my old life and we both know this will all soon die down. My life may never be the same as it was, but it will be pretty close. However, if the powers that be, decide they want to go after me and aggressively pursue a custodial sentence, then I may well have to spend my time once I'm released writing a full account of all that has happened."

"Eloise, are you issuing threats again?"

"Perish the thought. By the way, it must be a very busy time for the headline makers, because John Kuria has hardly had a mention."

Her elegant face produced the smuggest smile he could recall seeing. Still playing us then, he thought to himself.

"All I can tell you is that I will be playing things straight and true. My job is to prepare the charges for whatever crimes you've committed and then someone else decides if we should follow them through. If I'm leaned on to do anything else I will step aside."

"Thanks Graeme."

"I'm not sure we will ever agree about how good our justice system is though. I have done this job for a long while and seen some really bad men put away, and that was in spite of the money they had behind them. Most criminals get their just desserts in my view. I've had frustrations of course, but will we ever get it to a point where it's perfect?"

"I must show you the amount of messages I've got, mostly from mothers, who talk about being denied justice. Some are heart breaking. One woman wrote from prison as she had gone vigilante to gain the justice she wanted. She will never hug her daughter again, but the dealer who sold her child poison, wrapped up as the drug of her choice, will not recover from the knife attack. She felt his sentence was too lenient. Drug dealing can fund some very good lawyers, apparently, and his brief managed to persuade the judge that this was a remorseful man, touched by these events and keen to start a new life for himself away from the world of narcotics. He was so repentant that after the sentence was passed down and he was being led away, he turned to wink at this lady. So, she promised herself, and her daughter, that he would not walk the streets a free man. She attacked him on the day he was released from prison. In court she found out it was likely he died from her second blow, as it penetrated his heart, but she didn't know that and by the time she was dragged off him, there were a further 37 stab wounds. Will we ever get to the point where our justice system is perfect? Definitely not.........if we don't at least try."

CHAPTER 32.

Let your hair down;
To behave more freely than usual and enjoy yourself
This idiom originated in the 17th century, when women were expected to
wear their hair up in public, either in a bun, pinned on their head or in
elaborate styles. The only time they could let their hair down was for washing
or brushing, or when they were alone at home and could relax.

With no real reason to detain her, Eloise Langley had her passport returned and she was allowed to leave police custody. She was no danger to anyone and there was no appetite to take her on in court pursuing a custodial sentence, because the chances of winning against her impressive team of lawyers was not looking so great. Had she admitted to being party to a murder? No. Had she actually threatened anyone? No. She had wasted a lot of time for people who could be spending it much better elsewhere, but there was a growing wave of public support for her stance. Take her to court without being sure of a result and that could easily turn into a tsunami. Also, there was political and senior police pressure to get this matter over as quickly as possible. With their monopoly on hindsight, the journalists would crawl over every decision made and wantonly throw around accusations of evading responsibility, kowtowing to a celebrity and cowardice. The longer the case rolled on, the longer the whiff of all these would be allowed to linger.

* * *

The flight had been OK and she was so pleased to have Andrew for company on the journey. They watched a movie on his tablet, had a race to finish a Sudoku puzzle and then read some magazines. Nine and a half hours is a lot of time to fill, so his youthful energy and the ease with which he would become bored meant it relatively sailed by as they found things to do to keep him from being totally fed up. Their taxi ride was only thirty-five minutes and as it approached the marina, they spotted Bob and Alana waiting for them. Eloise kissed Bob, swept up Alana in her arms and then hugged her husband like she was never going to let him go.

They made their way onto the Yacht and threw the luggage down. Bob invited Andrew to join Alana and him on a shopping expedition and he eagerly agreed. He was looking forward to spending some time with his dad and, who knows, there might be a gift coming his way. Halfway down the walkway, Bob threw the car keys to Andrew and told them both to wait in the car for him. He turned back. He wanted a few precious moments with his wife.

"You OK?"

"Yeah. How well did your computer wizardry work? The PMs niece was genius."

"It did work well, but you carry all the accolades for whatever it is we have achieved."

"It is going to take some time to see what, if anything, we have actually accomplished. But, we have opened up a national debate and now it is up to others to see if it will lead to anything substantial. We've done our bit."

"Eloise, I'm so proud of you. I love you so much."

"Right back at you."

"For Tobias."

"For Tobias."

They kissed again and then he ran to the car. Eloise was obviously tired and headed for the bed to have a lie down, before her family returned. As her head hit the pillow, she caught sight of a photo of Tobias they kept on the bedside table. It was a couple of years old, but they loved it because it was an unplanned snap that caught him laughing. It was so natural, so him.

In a split second the court case, the what could have happened and the reason she had done it all flashed through her mind with hurricane intensity. It was over. The time was right for some much needed personal release.

Eloise hugged the pillow and cried.

JUST BEFORE YOU GO...

Thank you for reading Justice Within.

I write, because I love to. My hope is that, what I write, you love to read.

Eddie

If you have any views, please share them through the contact page on my website at

www.eddienewell.com.

You can also leave a review on Amazon to help others.

* * *

DCI Graeme King is already working on an exciting new case. Leave your details at www.eddienewell.com on the contact page and I will keep you posted on any new books.

Eddie Newell

Printed in Poland
by Amazon Fulfillment
Poland Sp. z o.o., Wrocław